FIRESIDE
POPSICLES

"Twisted Tales Told by the Fire"

Brought to you by Fireside Press.

Denver, Colorado - Chicago, Illinois

"Fighting night with light since 2013!"

POPSICLES!

In the year 2014, many wonderful anthologies were released in the world of literature. This volume is one of them. It took one princess, **SHEILA HALL**, from the Kingdom of Denver, Colorado to rescue an unassuming writer, **M.C. O'NEILL**, from the bowels of Chicago, Illinois to devise a master plan and craft a tome of the weird, the absurd and the bizarre for a reader's enjoyment.

Dozens of writers, poets and an Industrial musician from every corner of the planet rushed to her call in order to treat a myriad of consumers to a book full of remarkable tales and intriguing plots that few people could find in a miasma of mainstream publishing and literary regurgitation. And so, the struggle continued.

FIRESIDE POPSICLES was forged on a great spring day to fight the forces of ennui and the predictable. From these roaring fires, a host of incredible works were crafted from the minds of brilliant authors to bring peace, justice and pure terror to the galaxy…

Many thanks to the legion of marvelous editors who have made this fine book of fiction possible:

Sheila Hall
M.C. O'Neill
Paula von Gupta
Juliet McThudd
Pappagallo Chang
Robert "Bob" Calamari
Chantal Poots
Kim Jong van Houten
Frances "The Stinkbomber" Mung
Baldur Sharples
Buster Kimono
Glasya "Armpit" Labolas
Raymond Agamemnon
Ensor Toronto
Zara D'Lemma
Hunk Pumpwell
Suki Satanika
Odin Grundle
Nicole "Butt" Scratch
George Lincoln Lincoln
Merlin Ertel
Jennifer "Stop touching my ass, you dick" Pineapple
Arthur Congaline
Octavian Rodriguez
Dick Salvia
Roberta Saliva
Danger McPowell
Giuseppe Washington
Callista Zzyzzx
Anatoly Hartoonian
D.M.T. Jones
Biff McCheddar
Kim Un Hung

If we forgot any of you, well – we forgot you.

Dedicated to the fabulous Colonel Raye Roeske and her Daddy Bunny.

Cover art copyright 2013: *Popsicle Mayhem* by Hauke Vagt.

Jacket design by M.C. O'Neill.

Table of Contents

PAGE ONE!

We at Fireside Press suggest you not turn any more pages.
They are full of monsters...

Fireflies

Trevor Neale

Fireflies flit

Flickering images spit

From the flames

Playing mind games

Of dreams nocturnal

A yearning eternal

Under silken awning

These tales adorning…

Turn the pages of your mind

Inside out, unconfined to find

This cutting blade scything

Stories played to your writhing

Timeless, ancient and modern

Hot and moist, bloodied and sodden

All drowned in the mysterious

A virtuality so imperious…

Come aboard this rollercoaster ride

I dare you to fall into this fireside.

Trapdoor People or: The Birthsong of the Trapdoor Reborn

Douglas Hackle

There are two types of people in the world: regular people and trapdoor people.

Regular people never fall through trapdoors never to be seen or heard from again.

A trapdoor person, on the other hand, eventually falls through a trapdoor never to be seen or heard from again.

Trapdoors can open up anywhere and at any time. At residences, offices, schools, restaurants, places of worship, on the sidewalk, on the bus, in the bathtub - and yes, even on the toilet. After a person plummets into the darkness of one of these inexplicable apertures, the trapdoor immediately snaps shut like a deftly executed magic trick. Witnesses to this common spectacle are only ever afforded a quick glimpse of the starless black sea that some folks call "the trapdoor void."

Everyone in the world is considered a "regular person" until the moment a person falls through such a trapdoor. It does not happen to everyone. When and if a trapdoor will open up beneath any given person's feet is impossible to predict. Presumably, one can never know if one is a trapdoor person until the moment one ¬falls through. But even then, is a trapdoor person aware of what happens at the moment he or she disappears? We don't have an answer to this question because, much like death itself, no one has ever returned from the "other side" of a trapdoor. What's more, there's no historical record of a trapdoor person ever crying out or even pulling a scared face at the moment of the plunge. In fact, it is widely believed that trapdoor people experience complete bodily paralysis just as the ground unfolds beneath them.

My mother was a trapdoor person. Mere moments after she squeezed me out into a weary world plagued by war, disease, mindless consumerism, political corruption, prepubescent suicide bombers, all manner of douchebaggery, and people-eating trapdoors, she fell through a body-length trapdoor right there in her birthing bed in her hospital room. I know this only because my dad told me about it when I was six, moments before he too plummeted through a trapdoor that opened up on our living room sofa.

Yes, Dad was a trapdoor person too.

***

Nothing differentiates a regular person from a trapdoor person, so that the phenomenon of trapdoor disappearances appears random—again, not unlike death itself. For example, a man might live to be one hundred years old and, at the moment just before the expiration of his final breath, the centenarian might fall through a trapdoor that opens smack-dab in the middle of his deathbed. Similarly, a mother can give birth to a healthy 8.2-pound bundle of joy only to watch as some invisible force wrenches the newborn from the nurse's arms just as that nurse bends down to hand the baby to its mother; the infant sucked into a small trapdoor in the floor of the maternity ward, a trapdoor that slams shut just as suddenly as it opened.

And a natural, trapdoor-unrelated demise does not necessarily save one from this fate. Established in 1951, the International Center for Trapdoor Disappearance Research (ICTDR) conducted an experiment in the late 1960s in which infrared cameras were installed inside hundreds of buried coffins belonging to the recently deceased and long interred alike. The experiment demonstrated that sometimes trapdoors open up along the length of coffin bottoms, proving that the dead can be "trapdoored" just as effectively, mysteriously, and randomly as the living.

Even buried urns of cremated ashes are not immune to the ostensibly insatiable hunger of trapdoors.

***

In addition to taking both my parents, trapdoors have claimed several of my friends over the years, as well as a handful of cousins, aunts, uncles, several coworkers, and an untold number of acquaintances—not to mention my fiancé.

I even lost my barber to a trapdoor.

Sal Salerno was the old man's name. Old Mr. Salerno had cut my hair ever since I was a child. Grumbling on about how things were better back in the days when girls were girls and men were men, Old Sal was half-finished giving me a clip one day when he finally fell through—scissors, comb, and all. The old man didn't have any employees, so I was forced to exit his barbershop looking like a crazy person who had attempted to cut his own hair. By the time I had made it over to Best Cuts on the other end of town, I received more than a few funny looks while waiting for the traffic lights to turn green.

But these are the times we live in, and such stories are so common as to be almost uninteresting.

***

The first trapdoor disappearance on official record occurred February 7, 1945, just outside the city of Königsberg in what was then the German province of East Prussia. It had happened during the infamous evacuation of East Prussia just prior to the advancing Red Army's assault on that province. In broad morning daylight, a group of nearly thirty refugees that included both civilians and military personnel witnessed a trapdoor open in the muddy road directly beneath the feet of a seven-year-old girl named Bruna Johanna Holtzmann, who fell through the resulting black square in the same instant. The astonished refugees rushed to her aid, thinking the girl had fallen into a bunker or maybe booby trap set by the Soviets. With their hands, sticks, and knives they dug frantically and deeply into the mud, but to no avail.

Soon afterwards, trapdoor disappearances began to be witnessed and reported all over the world.

***

When I was in my early twenties, my best friend Kyle and I were barreling down the interstate in his fully restored '71 Dodge Charger after the bars had closed one Friday night, passing a big blunt back and forth. With Primus blaring from the back speakers in a steady, percussive blur of bass and drums, we were flying at close to a hundred miles per hour, not really caring if we lived or died, when Kyle and the half-spent doobie that was pinched between his thumb and forefinger dropped through the driver's seat—his obnoxious, howling laughter cut off just as abruptly as the rest of his physical existence.

For a moment, I stared in drunken, hazy disbelief over at the now-empty driver's seat as the decelerating muscle car began to list toward the median. In a panic, I swung my leg over to the driver's side floor, jammed my foot down on the brake, grabbed onto the veering steering wheel, but not before the car dove into the depression of the grassy median and hit an incline, sending me skyward. Somehow, I had managed to maintain control of the car as it landed and skidded to a tire-popping stop on the other side of the highway. I'm lucky the car didn't flip.

The cops at the scene wanted to pin me with a DUI. To this day, a somewhat common excuse among drunks who cause car accidents is to claim that they were in fact passengers in their own cars, and that the missing driver—who the drunk invariably describes as a nameless acquaintance met at the bar early that evening—disappeared through a trapdoor while at the wheel, forcing the drunk to take back control of his vehicle to save his own life and potentially the lives of others. But in my case, that is what really happened more or less.

Kyle was officially pronounced missing a couple days later, thereby corroborating my story. The DUI charge was dropped.

That was one small, good thing I suppose.

***

All international and national statistical and census systems incorporate "trapdoor disappearances" alongside the more traditional categories of births, deaths, fetal deaths, marriages, divorces, etc. According to the World Health Organization, on average, 8.3 percent of the global population disappears every year as a result of the trapdoor phenomenon. This percentage, which excludes post-burial trapdoor disappearances (i.e. "coffin cases"), has been fairly consistent since the mid-1950s, when reporting of global trapdoor disappearances first became coordinated.

There have been anomalous years. For example, the percentage jumped to over ten percent in 1976, while 1997 saw a drop to under three percent. But typically, it's just over eight percent every year.

Which is another way of saying one out of every twelve people in the world will become a trapdoor person.

***

Unfortunately for me, Stephanie Percinski, my high school sweetheart and bride-to-be, was a one-in-twelve.

We were as close to being married as anyone can possibly be when it happened, literally standing at the altar. I had just blurted, "I do." It was Steph's turn. She got as far as "I—." You can guess what happened next.

Picture me standing in front of three hundred friends and family members, me in my dapper tux—all nervous and awkward and hopelessly in love—me holding on to a third of my life savings in the form of a 1.3-carat, princess-cut diamond ring in my clenched right hand, my nervousness dissolving into disbelief and then into horror as I stared down at the empty space where my bride had just stood a moment ago in all her perfect, snow-white, gossamer-veiled, blushing beauty.

Gone forever.

***

The world's governments and global scientific communities have always been at a loss to explain the trapdoor phenomenon. But they try.

In 1997, as part of its fruitless, yet continuing research endeavors, the ICTDR began passing out special wristwatches to participating volunteers as part of a new study. These watches contained two-way microwave transmitters, functioning much like cell phones. The devices also emitted a constant, beacon-like shortwave radio signal separate from the manually activated voice transmission function. During the years in which the wristwatch program was active, participants signed contracts to wear one of these watches for a period of exactly one year. As long as the volunteers had kept the watches on their wrists during the course of the one-year contract, they were paid $500. The contracts automatically renewed if they were not breached. A participant in the program could remove his or her wristwatch at any time, but doing so was breach of contract and resulted in forfeit of pay and expulsion from the program. Trip mechanisms built into the watch bands alerted the ICTDR whenever a participant removed his or her wristwatch.

The idea was that if enough people were tagged with these devices, eventually some of them would fall through trapdoors. Perhaps then they could communicate with us from "the other side" as it were. At the very least, maybe we would be able to detect their beacon signals and trace the origin of the transmissions, thereby allowing us to discover the physical location of the trapdoor void, if such a thing even existed. The ICTDR monitored the airwaves for the wristwatch transmissions via its three large-dish radio telescopes, one located just outside of

6

Belfast, Northern Ireland, another near Cametá, Brazil, and the third in Cape Adare, Antarctica.

Since participants in the program were in no greater danger of falling through a trapdoor than nonparticipants, there was little reason not to sign up, so that the ICTDR succeeded in distributing its first 10,000 wristwatches in less than a week. Subsequently, thousands more people from around the globe signed up for the program.

Including yours truly.

***

A number of famous people have become trapdoor people. The ever-growing list includes Charles de Gaulle, Thomas Jefferson, Julie Andrews, Kareem Abdul Jabbar, Henry Winkler, Arsenio Hall, Nancy Reagan, Chelsea Clinton, Ice Cube, Nora Roberts, Daryl Hall, Crispin Glover, James Spader, The Edge, Wesley Snipes, Dakota Fanning, Jaden Smith, Stephen Hawking, Johnny Cash, Betty White, Vin Diesel, two of the Gosselin sextuplets, Bobby Blotzer (the drummer from Ratt), and both Charlotte and Emily Brontë (of the three sisters, only Anne was spared the trapdoor).

And that's just to name a random few.

***

Initially, the results of the ICTDR wristwatch program were discouraging. The first couple thousand people who fell through trapdoors while wearing the watches disappeared without a trace just like anyone else. No voice transmissions were subsequently received from these people, and the beacon signals of their watches simply ceased to be at the moment the watches disappeared through the trapdoors. Consequently, the ICTDR began phasing out the wristwatch program in 2008. Participants already enrolled in the program were paid at the expiration of their contracts, but no existing contracts were renewed, nor were any new contracts issued thereafter.

However, the ICTDR continued to monitor the radio waves just in case something should happen with any of the hundred thousand or so wristwatches that were still being worn in the general population or any of the thousands of wristwatches that had already gone through to the other side.

Just in case.

***

At last, on the morning of May 16, 2009, ICTDR's three radio telescopes simultaneously received two brief wristwatch transmissions, both sent from the same unit.

The first transmission, received at 4:32 AM GMT, consisted of approximately 7.27 seconds of the unit's beacon pulse signal. The signal was distorted, so that certain encrypted data, namely the unique identification code indicating the wearer of the watch, was obscured. Still, based on its frequency and phase modulation signature, the signal was unequivocally sent from one of the lost wristwatches.

About five seconds after the first transmission ended, a second transmission was received from the same source. This transmission consisted of a low-frequency hum that, after twelve seconds, was joined by a second sound.

To this very day, many experts and non-experts alike believe that second sound to be a distorted voice. Partially masked by the accompanying hum, the second sound—like some spectral mumble-whisper emanating from deepest reaches of space—continued for 22.74 seconds before the transmission abruptly ended.

Experts from diverse fields—acoustical engineers, acousticians, linguists, cryptanalysts, radio astronomers, particle physicists—have been analyzing that second transmission for decades now, but no one has been able to prove conclusively that the eerie, unintelligible noise is a voice, let alone offer some sort of conjectured translation of what the "voice" might be saying.

Lack of answers from the scientific community have only served to stoke the collective imagination of the public. Many believe the sound is the voice of an alien intelligence, and that the government knows this but seeks to hide the truth. Conspiracy theories abound. Others think the sound is the trapdoor dead themselves—a chorus of them singing from beyond the grave. Other folks are certain the sound is the Holy Voice of Yahweh, Allah, Vishnu, Shiva, Bondyè, etc. In a slightly less fantastical explanation, others believe the sound is the voice of that still-unidentified and perhaps still-living person—the owner and wearer of the detected wristwatch—and that the person's voice is simply distorted by whatever ether or medium or exotic space-time curvature that might characterize the place in which he or she is still trapped.

ICTDR's state-of-the-art directional finding equipment was unable to pinpoint a unique direction for either of the two transmissions; incredibly, the signals appeared to radiate from all directions in a manner similar to the transmission of the cosmic microwave background radiation observed throughout the expanding shell of the universe.

Since then, the radio telescopes have not received another wristwatch transmission.

***

That cryptic, inexplicable, spectral sound in the second transmission . . . it *is* a voice.

And it would not be entirely inaccurate to label it as the voice of an alien intelligence. Nor would it be erroneous to call that sound a choral deathsong of the trapdoor dead. Nor, for that matter (though the public never conceived of, or at least never widely embraced such a notion), would it be wrong to call the sound the birthsong of the trapdoor reborn. And that transmitted voice, in a certain manner of speaking, is indeed, and without a doubt, the Voice of Yahweh, Allah, Vishnu, Shiva, Bondyè, and all other human conceptions of the godhead. All of these explanations are simultaneously valid.

Not only am I certain the sound is a voice, but I happen to know exactly what the voice said—I know each and every astounding, staggering word uttered in that enigmatic 22.74-second transmission.

How do I know all this?

I know this because the transmission was sent from my wristwatch.

It's me who's talking and shouting and whispering and singing and whistling and laughing and weeping and panting and screaming in that transmission.

You see, I'm a trapdoor person too.

A Moment of Silence

Max Booth III

When somebody lives alone, they don't really pay attention to the sound of their voice. They barely even talk. Especially when they work from home on the computer, where all their conversation comes from typing on the keyboard. And even when they do talk, it isn't significant enough to give it a second thought.

Richard discovered he had lost his voice early in the morning, along with the rest of the world. He had just finished outlining his next column due to *Dark Moon Digest*, and was heading into the kitchen for a quick refill on coffee. His pinkie toe had always been an issue, even since infancy. So had the bottom corner of the wall, separating the living room and kitchen.

Whoever had designed that goddamn apartment was a masochist.

The coffee mug escaped from his grasp, shattering into a million little pieces all over the floor. His neck bent back, Adam's apple poking strongly against his neck, and his mouth opened wide as it released a scream similar to that of a banshee's. Afterward, he stood there for a moment, looking at all the broken glass, wondering if he'd startled any of his neighbors. He hoped nobody came knocking at his door—or, worse, called the police. He had deadlines to meet. There wasn't time for any of that nonsense.

Limping, he gathered a broom and dustpan and cleaned up the mess. He decided to forget the coffee. It was obviously cursed.

Richard sat back down at his MacBook and began reviewing his outline again, making sure he hadn't missed any glaring holes. He was still a little tense about a possible knock or phone call in regards to his obnoxiously loud screaming. He didn't want to deal with that. Maybe nobody heard it. Maybe nobody cared.

It was then that he realized that he hadn't actually screamed. Sure, his mouth had opened, and his vocal cords had strained with pressure, but no sound had left his mouth. Was he sure, though? Maybe, maybe not. It seemed ridiculous that the scream wouldn't have been audible.

Ridiculous, he tried to say, but he did not *hear* himself say it.

What the hell?

The words could only travel as far as his thoughts could take them.

This is wrong, something is wrong.

He opened his mouth again, tried to say "*Testing, testing,*" but heard nothing.

Am I deaf? Oh my God, I'm deaf.

No. That was impossible. He'd heard the coffee mug shattering. He could hear the traffic outside. Birds at his window. Planes in the sky. He could hear it all.

All but himself.

So, I'm mute, then?

His lips parted, tried to say *"Hello? Help! HELP!"* but he only hurt his lungs from trying too hard.

This is fucked, this is so fucked.

He stood up abruptly, pushing the chair to the ground behind him, and made for the cell phone plugged in at the counter. He held it in his hand for a moment, just staring at it. What was the point? He couldn't talk. Nobody would be able to hear him. It'd be like trying fill a bucket with water, only the bucket was missing a bottom.

Who would he call, anyway? He didn't know many people, and those he did know didn't particular care to speak to him anymore. He was divorced, his parents were dead, and all his friends had taken his ex-wife's side. He could call his agent. His agent always knew what to do. It was why Richard hired him.

Only the problem still remained: no voice, no reason to use the phone.

He was left with three options. He could hang back, try to wait whatever weird infliction this was out. Maybe it'd just go away after a while; kind of like hiccups. Second option, he could get on the MacBook, email his agent about what was going on. But who knew when he'd get a response? He could always try FaceBook. Make a random status declaring his lack of a voice—but how many of his social network friends would actually take him seriously? Besides, what would they know? The total intelligence of all his media contacts could be summed up with a badly spelled photo of an adorable kitten wearing a hat.

So that left the third option. He would have to leave his apartment, find someone else and try to mimic the situation. One of his neighbors, maybe; just keep pounding on the door until someone answered.

It was times like these that Richard felt like a lazy, horrible human being. He'd lived the last year and a half in this apartment; the whole time, sharing the same hallway with a deaf-mute. Not once had he ever bothered to even *attempt* to learn sign language. If there was anyone that would know what was going on, it'd be Hautala down the hall. Trying to converse with him now would just be useless.

It's always the actions you neglect that ends up killing you in the end.

Richard paused for a moment, standing there in his empty apartment. Outside on the street below, traffic carried on like normal. Everything continued. Nothing ever stopped.

Suddenly, a loud bang, like metal smacking metal, killed the tranquil silence. Richard jumped back, bumping his head against the wall. *What the hell was that?* He ran across his apartment to the opened window overlooking the city. He stuck his head out and scanned the streets below.

"Holy shit," he tried to say, but failed.

Car after car had flipped over and crashed into other cars, piled up on top of each other. Drivers, passengers and random pedestrians ran around the wreckage like chickens with their heads cut off. They stood in front of each other waving their hands like crazy.

It occurred to Richard that even though he could hear car alarms barking like mad, he couldn't actually hear anything else. Even from how high he stood in his

11

apartment, he could still see everyone's mouths opening and closing. But nothing came out. They were just as silent as he was.

What the hell is going on?

Richard was done staying in his apartment. Either he had been stricken with a strange disorder that blocked all human vocals from entering his ears, or everybody had gone mute. It would be impossible to further self-diagnose until he had determine which one it was. Plus, that pile-up outside looked really bad. Somebody was bound to need some help.

He kicked on his shoes, threw a shirt on and headed out the door. He didn't even lock it behind him; suddenly, possessions no longer mattered. There were a few other people in the hallway, just walking around aimlessly, but Richard didn't pay them any mind as he pushed past and ran to the elevator.

It was the longest ride of his life. His heart beat loudly against his chest with every nauseous movement it made downward. For a moment, he found it amusing that he could hear his own heart but not his voice. The humor in it quickly diminished, however.

Outside, the alarms of the wrecked cars were much louder. The noise pierced his eardrums; it made his teeth hurt. People were running past him in both directions, hands waving in the air, mouths open wide, yet with absence of a voice. Blood stained the streets. Corpses hung limp through shattered car windows. This was madness. What had happened? Where were the police, the ambulances? Hadn't anyone called them?

Of course nobody had. Phones were useless now. Conversation had suddenly become obsolete.

Without the use of their tongues, everybody had become helpless.

Dear God, how many people is this affecting?

An Asian man with a messenger bag stumbled up to him, mouth going a mile a minute. Richard shrugged. He didn't know what else to do. The Asian began tapping his wristwatch furiously. Richard shrugged a second time and the man gave up, angry, and ran away.

A woman lay in the street, half her body pinned underneath a flipped car. Her stomach was smashed to hell and her guts were spattered all over the street around her. She was reaching out toward God, mouth unhinged for a silent scream.

How the hell could this pile-up have happened? This was utter insanity. He was surrounded by corpses and obliterated metal. Richard tried to imagine it; maybe two people had been conversing in their car, when suddenly they both realized neither one could hear the other. In the midst of the confusion, the driver took his or hers eyes off the road and ran a red light, getting plowed by traffic. Maybe the same thing happened to two dozen different cars at the same time. Three dozen, a hundred, a thousand.

Or maybe something else happened. There were an infinite number of possibilities and Richard would never know the truth. He didn't *want* to know the truth. He just wanted it to end.

A crying child tugged at his shirt. He looked down and tried to smile, but failed. Instead, he waved sadly.

The child was asking him something, but he didn't have any idea what it was. Maybe asking where her mother and father were. He looked back at the dozens of corpses littered across the street and quickly turned back to the child. He brushed a finger through her hair, and she flinched back, biting his hand.

Richard pulled away quickly, holding his bitten hand and watching as the confused child fled the scene.

This was all happening so fast, and he had no idea what to make of it.

Richard approached a woman sitting down on the curb. Her face was covered in blood and she was weeping. Tears fell down her cheeks, mixing with the blood, but no sound escaped her lips. She took no effort to hide her despair. Why should she?

He leaned down and placed a hand on her shoulder and she let her head fall into his chest. He wrapped his arms around her, embracing her with his warmth. It didn't matter that her blood and tears rubbed against his shirt. With a hundred humans surrounding them, panicking without making a sound, nothing at all mattered.

Richard watched as two men attempted to argue with each other. They both were opening their mouths, trying to scream at the other one, but nothing was out. Their faces strained with stress and frustration. Their bodies trembled with pure rage. Richard had no idea what had sparked the argument; maybe they had crashed into each other during the pile-up, or maybe they were just trying to figure out what had happened to their poor, precious voices. Either way, a solution was not being made, and it didn't take long before one of the men to lash out physically at the other.

Flesh against flesh, violence upon violence, the two men tumbled to the bloodstained street with fists whirling like murderous perpetual motion machines. The sound of their faces being brutalized was louder than Richard could have ever expected; it made his stomach nauseous, and if he hadn't been holding a strange woman, he would have surely vomited. Yet he couldn't take his eyes off the scene. One of the men stayed on top of the other, repeatedly pounding his knuckles into the man's face despite the fact that the man on the ground was long dead. He kept trying to scream at his corpse, and the more he failed, the more he cried, the more he lashed out.

He got up from the dead man and approached someone else who was trying frantically to talk on a cell phone. The man grabbed a hold of the Cell Phone Man's neck and began to squeeze, again screaming something nobody else could hear.

Richard imagined he was saying, *"They can't hear you, you stupid fuck! Just hang up already, because nobody can hear you! Don't you REALIZE that? WE ARE ALONE!"*

Richard looked away, and held the woman tighter against his chest.

This is crazy, he thought, *this is so goddamn crazy, I don't even know where to begin.*

What were they supposed to do? Life as they knew it was crumbling beneath their feet faster and faster. More life was destroyed as each second ticked by. How could anyone be expected to continue as they had before? They couldn't talk, they couldn't communicate. They couldn't call an ambulance, they couldn't call a loved one.

Five miles away, Richard watched as two airplanes collided into each other. There was a bright, vibrant explosion that made everyone stop what they were doing and watch it, eyes wide with horror. The flames lingered in the sky for what felt like eternity.

The whole world had completely shut down.

Why?

Richard shook his head, discouraged. Wondering "why" on something as insane as this would be useless. He might as well have wondered what had brought them to this planet in the first place. How could anyone possibly answer something like this?

This was … this was lunacy.

And lunacy had no answer.

***

Richard led the woman back up to his apartment. She did not seem hesitant to follow—if anything, she was eager to escape the massacre happening on the streets. Any place would be safer compared to that hell. He showed her to the couch and she sat down while he fetched her a soda from the fridge. She nodded her thanks and gulped it half down, like she'd been dying of dehydration. Her body shivered violently. Richard handed her a blanket and she took it, smiling sadly. The woman watched every move Richard took, as if afraid of what he'd do when she wasn't looking.

He didn't blame her. After what had happened outside, anything was possible.

He sat down on the sofa next to her, wishing he could tell her that it was okay, that they were safe up here. But all he could do was just sit there like an idiot. How long could they stay like this, he wondered, before they would have to begin thinking of a plan of action?

How long would she stay?

Richard grabbed a notebook laying on the coffee table and wrote at the top of a new page: "*Hello, my name is Richard.*"

He handed her the pen, and she wrote below, "*What is happening?*"

"*I don't know,*" Richard wrote.

"*Why can't we talk?*" she asked, and he tapped the line above for an answer. Then she wrote, "*I'm scared.*"

"*Me too.*"

He looked the woman deep in the eyes, sharing the same tears. Her face was still smeared with dried blood. It looked awful. He felt so bad for her; there was this urge in him that wanted to take care of her forever.

"Is it going to stop?" she asked.

"God, I hope so."

"I want to go home," she wrote.

Richard placed a hand on her thigh, and wrote, *"It is safe here. I promise."*

He leaned forward, kissed her lightly on the lips. She flinched.

She was still scared. No doubt still thinking about the madness out on the street. How could you not?

He picked the notebook back up and wrote, *"DON'T LEAVE,"* underlining *"LEAVE"*.

He headed for the bathroom and closed the door behind him, which was a rarity when you lived alone. Richard took out his phone and stopped again, reminding himself that he couldn't call anyone. Would he ever be able to again? He wish he knew the answer.

He logged onto FaceBook briefly to see what everyone else was saying about this most unfortunate event. His newsfeed wall was corrupted with picture after picture of overused meme; cats in humorous positions, children smoking cigarettes, dogs with sunglasses on their tails. The only actual status that he found was an old co-worker saying that he was hungry. Richard sighed and returned the cell phone to his pocket.

He took care of his business quickly, then found a washcloth in the cupboard that he damped with hot water. He grabbed a box of bandages and headed back into the living room to take care of the woman's head wound, only to find that she was gone from the couch and now heading for the front door.

Where the hell was she going?

He tossed the washcloth and bandages on the table and rushed over to stop her, grabbing her shoulder and spinning her around. He smiled innocently at her, shrugging as if to ask what was going on. What was she thinking, trying to go back out in that chaos?

She opened her mouth to scream a soundless scream. Richard held her tighter, trying to understand what she was trying to convey.

Goddammit, if we could just talk...

The door to his apartment suddenly burst open, having been kicked in by the murderous madman from the street. The one who'd brutally beaten the men outside. Why of all apartments, why had he chosen this one?

There was no time to question the situation; the situation had already arrived full-force.

The woman leaped out of the way and the madman tackled Richard to the floor. He could feel the air being pushed from his body and he desperately tried to reclaim it with little success. The madman was on top of him, just as he had been on the man down on the street—the dead man he had brutally slaughtered with his bare hands.

The madman raised his fist and slammed it into Richard's face. He could feel a stream of warmness flow down his cheek. *Jesus Christ, what was wrong with this guy?*

Richard watched in horror as the madman raised his fist again, only this time Richard managed to move his head out of the way just before contact was made. He used this slight advantage to grab a hold of the madman and fling him off to the floor. Richard scrambled to his feet, picked up a barstool by the kitchen counter and swung it around just as the madman was standing back up. The hard wood of the seat cracked loudly against the side of the madman's skull and he immediately collapsed to the ground, body limp. A puddle of blood quickly formed underneath his head.

"Holy shit, holy shit," Richard tried to say, *"I just killed him."*

He dropped the stool and just stood there for a moment. He had never killed someone before. He had gone his whole life thinking he would never have to, and yet, now he had, and it could never be taken back.

Dear Lord, what has happened to the world?

The woman slowly walked out of the kitchen, from her hiding spot, looking at the corpse in utter horror. Her whole body was shaking. In her hand she gripped a large steak knife.

"It's okay now," Richard wanted to say, *"the bad man is gone."* He held out his arms, hoping that she'd embrace him.

Embrace him she did.

He didn't realize the steak knife was in his stomach until he was lying on the ground, looking at the ceiling. Suddenly, there was a pain deep in his gut, and everything felt warm and wet.

What? Why?

No ...

The woman stood above him for a moment, crying. Then she turned around and ran out of the apartment, leaving him to die with the man he had just killed.

Had he frightened her that badly? Jesus Christ, he was just trying to protect them. Why would she do such a thing after he'd saved her life? What was *wrong* with her?

Now he was going to die, too, and for *what?* How utterly meaningless of an ending. He hadn't done anything wrong. He was a good person, dammit. He didn't deserve this.

Body growing numb, he discovered a cell phone on the carpet beside him. Weakly, he picked it up and looked at the screen. It must have belonged to the dead madman next to him. He wouldn't need it any longer.

Richard looked at the screen. It was a series of text messages from the madman and a woman named Laura.

ME: "Where the hell did u go?"

LAURA: "A man took me."

ME: "What man???"

LAURA: "Idk. He just took me."

ME: "WHERE??"

LAURA: "The building outside. Apartment 5B."

ME: "I'm on my way."

LAURA: "Help me. He's in the bathroom but I think he's going to rape me. Please hurry."

Richard threw the cell phone across the room. It exploded against the wall. His gut felt like it was on fire.

He began to laugh, and he did not stop for a very long time, despite the fact that no sound left his mouth.

***

He passed out. When he came to, he heard singing. A man. Not on the radio either, but somebody inside his apartment.

Somebody was singing.

Richard stirred into a sitting position, grabbing at his bleeding stomach. The pain was immense, like the ocean.

There was a man in the kitchen, going through his cabinets. The man took out a bag of sugar and turned around, startled to see that Richard was awake.

Richard looked at the man a good while. He recognized him.

It was the deaf-mute from down the hall. Hautala.

And he'd been *singing.*

What in the hell?

"Oh, hello there," the deaf-mute said. "I hadn't realized that you were actually alive, sorry about that. You see, I made tea, but clumsy me forgot to buy sugar this week. I trust it's okay if I go 'head and borrow some?"

Richard shrugged. Nodded.

Hautala grinned from ear-to-ear. "Excellent! Thank you very much, friend. I went ahead and called an ambulance for you, but there wasn't exactly much of a response on the other side. It sure is quite the day, is it not?"

Richard just looked at him. This wasn't happening.

Hautala grinned again. "Well, I guess I'll be off. There is just so much left to accomplish, now that … well, you know. God, for the first time in my life, it feels *good* to be alive!"

He didn't just walk out the door, but skipped. Singing the whole time.

Just as he entered his own apartment down the hall, Richard heard the deaf-mute shout, "Thanks again for the sugar!"

How Billy Bob Jones Changed the World

Pedro Proença

Young Billy Bob Jones was born into a happy, loving family. His father, Jimmy Bob Jones, was a landfill tycoon. He rose from poverty by cleaning up other people's messes. He had built himself a multi-million dollar empire, from the ground up, on his own. Built it with sweat and tears.

And trash. Lots of trash.

Ol' Jimmy Bob liked mansions. He hired the best architects of the world to build several grand mansions in various cities. His favorite, and where he spent most of his time with his family, was in the city he'd built, Jimmytown. Seeing the struggles of the poor, who constantly scavenged his landfills in search of some food or recycling products to sell for pennies, Jimmy Bob Jones built a city to house these people, free of charge, around his biggest landfill in South America. His mansion was built *inside* the landfill.

I should mention that Jimmy Bob was clinically insane.

The Jones family had a predisposition for benign brain tumors, that usually caused peripheral damage to the one inflicted. Some of his predecessors were blind, some were deaf.

Jimmy Bob's craziness was mostly harmless. He liked to sing naked in his mansion's halls, and he would occasionally show up to Billy Bob's school, nude, his man boobs dangling, dripping with sweat, complaining to his son that the goblins had shit in the bathtub again. In spite of all that, Billy Bob loved his crazy, old dad.

Billy Bob's tumors had begun to appear when he was only a few months old. His brain damage was not anything as severe as his old man's. His damage was anosmia - the total loss of his sense of smell. Living in a house surrounded by garbage, this was a gift from the heavens for young Billy Bob.

When Billy Bob was twelve, the family doctor told his dad that the tumors needed to be removed, for they were growing, and that could cause even more damage to the boy's health. So, Jimmy Bob paid the top surgeons of the world to operate on his precious son.

The surgery was a success. Well, almost.

All of the tumors were removed, but they had left a permanent aberration to the olfactory nerve: All information from different smells was improperly evaluated by the brain. A smell Billy Bob's brain should consider "pleasant," was now perceived as "unpleasant," and vice versa. So, roses on a meadow, to Billy Bob, smelled like old dung from a rectal cancer-ridden cow.

Again, this proved fortuitous for Jimmy Bob's young heir, since he lived in a landfill. The bad side was that Billy Bob was confined to the interior of his father's mansion, and the landfill that surrounded it. He couldn't go to school like normal boys, because breathing pure, fresh air was excruciating to him. All that was needed was one clean whiff, and the smell of a bum's asshole would fill Billy Bob's nostrils.

To deal with the problem of his son's education, Jimmy Bob had hired several private tutors to teach his son everything he was required to learn at school. Their clothes needed to be dipped in garbage juice and human feces to wipe out all exterior scents that they might bring in to the mansion. To prevent projectile vomiting from the tutors, Jimmy Bob provided them with oxygen masks. And to prevent refusal, he provided them with lots and lots of money.

When he was eighteen, Billy Bob lost both of his parents. They were coming back home from a dinner party in Jimmy Bob's honor, when their car was struck by a truck. A garbage truck that belonged to Jimmy Bob's corporation.

That's irony for you, folks.

So, Billy Bob cried for days. His beloved family had been taken away from him. And the thought of being forever confined to this enormous, empty mansion tormented him. He decided to leave the mansion and travel the world. He gave up on the idea the moment he left the limits of his landfill's sweet aroma. He gagged and heaved, and went running back to his mansion.

"If I can't go out into the world, then I must do something to make my name known to everyone on Earth," Billy Bob said to himself. He felt a need to do something good, just like his father had done when he had built Jimmytown for the poor.

This was around the time the craziness had started to settle. For one tumor had begun to grow in Billy Bob's brain again; this time distorting his views on the world.

For the next ten years, Billy Bob secluded himself in a laboratory of his own design, trying to find a solution to some of the world's biggest problems.

When he finally found what he was looking for, he couldn't help thinking the idea was extremely simple. A simple idea, with a very complex execution.

Ten more years had passed. Billy Bob hired the most brilliant minds in engineering and science from all over the world to make his dream come true, his gift to the planet.

A press conference was called. Billy Bob Jones, secluded landfill tycoon, announced his plans to gather all of the earth's trash from its biggest landfills and send them into the sun, in specially designed containers, that would be propelled by newly invented unmanned rockets, all developed by his team of brilliant minds.

The whole world applauded. Soon, the containers started to collect all the trash from various landfills around the earth, including the one in Jimmytown. Billy Bob showed up to an interview in his mansion, wearing shit-covered clothes, saying he was happy to help the world and thrilled that his name would be put alongside men like Da Vinci, Galileo, Ford and Salk. All he wanted was to help everyone.

(I should note that, by this time, Billy Bob was already fully insane, but his goblins now shat on the living room rug, instead of in the bathtub).

Countdown:

10... 9... 8... 7... 6... 5... 4... 3... 2... 1...

Blast off!

The rockets flew simultaneously, sending the majority of the world's trash into space.

Well, that was the plan.

In mid-flight, every one of the rockets blew up. All of that garbage was put into Earth's orbit, turning our once-beautiful planet into a fetid rock floating in space.

Civilizations collapsed, people became savages fighting for their lives in this shit-smelling world. Oceans arose with the vomit of entire cities. Religious leaders announced that it was the Apocalypse, that all should repent now, before it was too late.

And in the midst of it all, Billy Bob Jones strolled through the streets, detonator in hand, breathing in as deep as he had ever done in his life.

Waves and the Darkness

Mercedes M. Yardley

Jeremy promised he would never leave me. That he'd be the only person in my life never to do so. I didn't know whether I believed him or not, not really. I'm sure he meant what he said, at least at the time. But things happen. Circumstances change. There isn't always a choice.

One time he told me that he was born with a darkness inside of him, that he didn't know how to make it go away. He wanted to hurt things, he said. He wanted to squeeze necks and break legs. Slash at throats. He told me how he watched the pulse in my neck. Kept time of its beating. After he mentioned this, I noticed how his eyes would wander to my throat, and his breathing would change. As if he were waiting for something. For my heart to stop. For my blood to coagulate inside of my veins, if it didn't spill out of them first. He wanted to press his thumb on my artery to see what would happen.

And I was somebody he loved. I don't want to know what he thought of those he didn't care for.

It wasn't ill-feeling. Not really. It wasn't that he hated. He just wanted to make everybody sorry.

"Sorry for what?" I asked him once. We were just kids, sitting on the rocks and staring into the ocean. I had my crying doll with me, back before Jeremy pulled off her head to see what kind of sound she made. I was never able to put her back together, but that was all right. I still had Jeremy.

"I don't know. Just sorry."

He wasn't dark all of the time, and that's what made the difference. The shadow would come in waves, nearly crushing him under the weight of despair, and then it would ebb out. He'd be charming and funny. Happy. This was the Jeremy I knew, the one I enjoyed. It didn't surprise anybody when we grew up and fell in love. Jeremy and Kat. It's just how it was always meant to be. That, and nobody else on the island really wanted either one of us. That's how it had already been, and that was just fine with us.

We'd sneak up to the old lighthouse some nights, playing tricks on the tourists and planning our future. We picked out a day to get married, not too far off but far enough, and made lists of the songs that we wanted to dance to after our wedding.

"Hey, Kat. You know I'll never leave you, right?"

I didn't say anything.

"We'll be together always. I promise you."

I smiled, and I swear it almost felt natural.

"I believe you, Jeremy. Really."

He knew better than that, I could see it in his eyes. But he also knew I was trying, and that's what mattered.

"I'll prove it to you, Kitty Kat. Just wait and see."

His smile was a beautiful thing. It filled me with hope. Sometimes with terror, deep down, but mostly something that I think was happiness.

"Jer? I love you. I do."

"I know you do. I love you, too."

And then Jeremy went dark. It was worse than usual, worse than I had ever seen. He wouldn't talk to me. Wouldn't let me touch him.

A little boy went missing from town and I was too terrified to ask him about it. He simply stared at the sea. It lasted for weeks this time.

"Please tell me what's wrong!" I begged him the last time that I saw him. "Why won't you let me help you?"

"Nobody can help me," he said. He wouldn't even look at me. I pulled my coat closer around me, the wind grabbing at my hair and trying to push me from the rocks.

"But we're getting married in eight days," I said. "Can't you at least try to act happy? Pretend that it matters to you?"

He didn't answer, and I turned and ran, tripping over the rocks and pieces of shell. He'd already left me, just like I was afraid he would. I had never been so angry. I'd never felt so alone.

The Coast Guard found Jeremy's body wedged between the underwater rocks near the shore. They barely recognized him, they said, because he was so bloated and discolored from the sea. We buried him on what was supposed to be our wedding day.

That night, I went dark as well. The feelings overwhelm me, this despair and anger and hatred, and I know that they aren't mine. I'll see a couple walking together, looking like they belong with each other, and I want to kill them, rend them apart because they are happy, and I never will be.

Jeremy won't let me. He follows me everywhere now. He's always prowling for somebody new to hurt. He smoothes my hair back when I sleep, and threatens everyone around me. My sister came to visit after his death, and he pushed her from the rocks. He appeared once in front of my father and caused him to have a heart attack. I dared to date a man, just once, and my date was killed in a car crash on the way home. Anybody that I talk to becomes his victim.

"I told you we'll always be together," Jeremy had said, and he meant it. He is cutting me off from everybody that I know, from everybody that can help me. He wants me to jump from the same rocks that he did and join him, and I'm afraid that it won't be much longer before I do.

I'm sorry; I shouldn't have told you all of this. I'm afraid that I have put you in danger. What? Of course he's here. He's sitting in that chair, right behind you.

He promised he would never leave me. I should have believed him.

Luna Too

James Ward Kirk

Block is a giant. Block's soul is diminished, however, so he slumps. His heart hurts and he sleeps on the floor of his home. His dark suit is tailored to fit, but doesn't, like the rest of him.

The murder scene is larger and bitterer than even Block. Blood will never completely be washed away from this kitchen. Some small part of this human sacrifice shall live here forever, even when the house is lost to time, some soft cell of her melting into the earth below, a specter eternal also haunting Block until he offers his mortality to the universe.

The esoterism of this woman, the parts that comprise the human body, are displayed for review. Next to each organ is a small yellow sign with a number embossed in black, quite in contrast to the red—but not all blood is red. Liver blood is as black as the ink, perhaps God's comment upon the human condition. The numbers run high as nothing much remains inside Mary's habitus.

The refrigerator kicks on.

Her eyes stare at Block from atop the refrigerator. Her face, deftly removed, is placed perfectly around the eyes. She seems more curious than angry. Her heart is in the sink, with fresh apples. Her intestines hang from the ceiling like sticky fly traps and are already at work. The buzzing is loud. The woman's brain is on the counter next to the microwave, split in half, and smells like fresh mushrooms.

Block's feet are too large for crime scene covers. He reaches into his jacket pocket and removes a roll of green-black thirty gallon plastic trash bags. He uses a shoestring to tighten one around each calf. He steps into the lake of blood, sending ripples like lunar tidal waves splashing against the floorboards. Block cannot avoid all the hanging entrails, and flies angry for being distracted form an anti-halo around his head. Congealed blood mixes with his hair, clings to his face and shoulder, and as he turns away, I imagine a tear forming in his eye.

Block imprints her pain upon his soul, incapable of not, of not knowing, not absorbing; like hovering near a loved one, a cancer patient, and listening to the final murmurs of life.

"This is the twelfth of the first," he says. His voice is as big as his body, and in the other room a paramedic begins weeping.

Block bends at the knees as if in prayer. He removes a tongue suppressor and gently pushes at the stomach; he sniffs gently at the cut esophagus and says, "Peppermint schnapps." *The girl was just having a little fun, perhaps a first date.*

The Coroner tells Block he shouldn't have done that and Block tells her to go fuck herself. Block will read the woman's report, words surgical and clean as if she is above human sentiment. He has absorbed the facts he needs from this theatre of the absurd.

Block walks to the edge of the kitchen and removes the bags from his feet. He steps into the hallway. People move away from him like sheep and he their Shepherd. "What is Mary's last name?" He knows her name is Mary. All twelve of these poor souls are named Mary.

"Benevolentia," the Coroner says, still new and unaware of the anger residing within Block.

"Mary Benevolentia," says Block.

The Coroner starts, "It means—"

"I know what it means," Block says. "It's Latin for 'good will'."

The Coroner enjoys the last word. "The subject's liver is in the refrigerator. The time of death is compromised."

No, though Block; *the time of life is compromised.*

Like his wife's, Luna, her face strangled purple-black with a scarf. Block places his right hand upon his chest. His heart hurts.

2.

Alexander Lystan is shopping for a silk scarf.

"For your wife?" asks the sales girl. She is perhaps twenty-six. Her red hair is the death of her.

No. For you. "Which scarf do you most enjoy?" Lystan is tan and thin and handsome. He is charismatic, like sunsets.

"That's easy," she answers, choosing a green scarf the color of spring grass. The Eiffel Tower is patterned into the silk scarf.

Lystan asks the girl for her name.

"Abby," she says. She has a card: Abby Grwanski.

How many Grwanski's are there in the phone book? he wonders. *Not many,* he thinks, and later he will find her on Facebook too.

Lystan gives the girl some cash and concludes his transaction. He neatly folds the receipt in half and places it in his wallet. Lystan has seventeen similar receipts at home pinned to his bedroom ceiling.

***

Lystan moves artfully toward his Vienne French four-poster bed. He is nude, semi-erect, and carries the scarf with him. He sighs as he lies down upon five thousand dollars in silk bedding. He ties the scarf tender and tight around his neck, a knot perfect for choking oneself. He takes his fully erect member in his right hand and begins strangling himself with the scarf with his left.

***

Lystan is not beaten as a child; he does not go hungry or want for things other children less fortunate than him envy. He is a bright and meticulous student and earns the praise of his teachers. Peers admire and like him, and seek his company and companionship. Girls want to kiss him.

He does not kill small animals. He loves Mother and Father.

He does not murder until one night, under a harvest moon, in the company of a young woman from a neighboring university—a spontaneous event while he is trolling the streets for pleasure.

Lystan is quite bored with life. He absorbs the information his professors offer effortlessly, and in a short time understands their areas of expertise perhaps even better than they. He is comfortable materially. Money is no problem for him. Mother and Father take good care of him, when they visit and when away. Lystan wants for nothing but his lust is overwhelming and sovereign. He does not work.

Lystan and Amanda are sitting in a white convertible, the top down, fondling one another and Lystan is unable to achieve an erection. An idle thought excites him: he might enjoy taking her life. He begins the process, uncertain at first, fumbling around until he discovers that he truly enjoys the eroticism of his hands upon the girl's delicate neck. His erectile dysfunction problem is solved as the natural life of the young woman flees him.

His orgasm is a life-changing event.

Sated, he looks about and finds no person has witnessed his murder. As he returns his attention to his date, he discovers the rub—moonlight reveals his fingerprints upon his lover's throat.

Lystan drags the young woman's corpse to a copse of fir trees and hides it there. He fumbles around in the dirt and comes upon a sharp rock and obliterates her throat and his fingerprints. Returning to his car he finds the woman's purse on the floorboard, and her red scarf. He uses the scarf to lift the purse, and his member stirs at the sensation of silk rubbing leather. He leaves the scarf and the purse beside the corpse.

The memory of the scarf elevates his spirits for several months. Then reminiscence is not enough.

Lystan researches serial killers. He does not delude himself. He understands his undertaking. The first to turn up on Google is the Green River Killer. He turns away in disgust. He will kill regular women. How nice to begin with a policeman's wife? He trolls the local newspaper online and reads about a giant.

***

Lystan sits up on the bed, frustrated. He cannot climax. He has a man in mind. The man's name is Alexander Mort. Mort is stealing his limelight.

Lystan and Mort kill in harmony one night, a year ago, albeit on opposite sides of town and each unaware of the other, and Mort gets the headlines. Television is all atwitter about the man named Mort. Mort is brutal. Lystan likes to think of himself as not inhuman. To discover his art regulated to the second page of the paper, a mere afterthought of reporters because of Mort, infuriates Lystan. He is chagrined that he and Mort share the same given name.

The police are bereft of information regarding Alexander Mort. Lystan is not. He has seen Mort. He has witnessed the work of Mort and explored the aftermath. Mort is a brutal, ugly and stupid man. Lystan has decided that if the police cannot locate Mort then he shall assist them. He has all of the necessary information.

Lystan decides he will visit the public library, access a public computer and send the giant all of the information he needs to apprehend Mort—all contained in a tidy email from a temporary account.

Lystan freshens up. He's decided one more night of surveillance is required before he greets his new lover Abby.

3.

Mort is comfortable in his lair. He lies upon an abandoned mattress.

He lives in an abandoned, stand-alone wood frame building once owned by a Russian who sold tobacco out the front door and heroin out the back door. He lives here alone having frightened away other would-be squatters with a simple meeting of the eyes. One man did not look away from Mort's eyes and died.

Mort is not retarded, as Lystan suspects, but he is brain damaged because of poor nutrition as an infant and repeated punches and kicks to the head as a toddler. He is self-aware.

Mort is good with his hands partly as a result of growing up on a farm in California and working construction as a teen. He has secured his home from would-be intruders. Police are content to leave it alone as the building's outward appearance resembles any other well-kept building closed because of the poor economy. The windows are covered with thick plywood. The doors are secured with premium locks. Drug dealers and prostitutes do not frequent the corner—and this *is* a surprise to local police. As one patrolman said of the surrounding neighborhood, "You can't throw a rock in this area without hitting a whore or a drug dealer." Mort does not tolerate people near the building, transient or not.

Mort often sleeps in the chicken coop as a child, especially when Mary has masculine visitors. Sometimes they stay awhile but eventually they all leave. He does not mind sleeping with the chickens. The mild cooing of the sleeping chickens calms him. The stench is preferable to that encountered in the house.

At age five Mort's mother takes him between her legs. Mort's penis is huge, but it is not his member that visits her dark place. He is awkward at first, and struggles for breath, but Mother That Becomes Mary is an excellent if cruel tutor.

At age eight, and beyond Mort's understanding, his member becomes tumescent when servicing Mary; Mary is outraged: "How dare you!" She lights a cigarette and burns his penis. Mort never experienced another erection after that, not even upon awakening or if needing urgently to urinate, but the burning of his penis continues. A ritual develops.

As a man, Mort's penis is scarred from base to tip. When he touches its leather-like surface to urinate, he becomes furious. A rage builds. The rage becomes frenzy. He uses a phone book to find Mary, and his wrath is released with Mary's death.

For a while; alas, the rage builds like the need for inhalation. Mort will find Mary again and she will die like an exhalation—spent. In death, Mary is Momma again.

Mort moves to a sitting position. He is troubled regarding the last Mary.

She says, as the knife descends, as its point penetrates, "I forgive you."

Several minutes pass before her words come to life in his thoughts, like a ghost ascending from its grave. He is sitting, a kidney in each hand, and he hears her words echo in his mind like the "who?" of an owl.

No one has said these words to Mort.

Standing behind Mary's house, hiding in the shadows of the alley, Mort says "I forgive you."

He looks back at the house and sees a man entering. Mort returns to the house and peers through a window. He sees a man standing there, holding a silk scarf. Mort gets to know this man named Lystan.

Mort stands and leaves the mattress. He urinates into a coffee can. He returns to his mattress and lies down again—and at that moment another voice cracks through his consciousness.

The voice says, "I am God. I forgive you."

Mort brings his hands to his head and says aloud. "Thank you, God." Mort has heard of God. He is a kind man who lives in heaven. Heaven is a nice place.

God says, "I demand recompense."

"What does 'recompense' mean, God?"

"You must give Lystan to the giant."

"Okay, God." Mort knows the giant. He always goes to Mary. Mort thinks the giant wants to put the Mary back together again, and this is fine because the Mary is now cleansed.

Mort rises, and begins the work God has given him. Crucifixion comes to mind.

4.

Lystan sits in his car outside Abby's apartment building. Abby's apartment is at ground level. Lystan is happy about this as it will make his entrance and exit less dangerous. There is a copse of maple trees behind the apartment complex and a small lake. As Lystan contemplates the subtleties of variance between suffocation by silk and drowning, he sees Mort leave the apartment carrying Abby.

Lystan understands this is no coincidence. Mort must have some plan. Lystan is not concerned. Mort is a brute, and it follows that his plans are brutish. He watches without agitation as Mort disappears into the woods behind the apartments. He wonders if Mort can get home without interference from the police. He imagines Mort making the trek home with success, as Mort enjoys at least the cunning of a coyote carrying its prey. He knows where Mort lives, and even has a master key for the locks there. Lystan is comfortable. He has planned their eventual congress of the two.

Lystan starts his car and leaves for Mort's den. He will wait in the rafters, like a bat.

5.

Block awakes from his slumber. The moon is bright for a moment, but then clouds move over like a sheet over a corpse. The floorboards beneath him creak as he rises to his feet, as do his bones.

Block has not slept upon his bed since Luna died.

He's hungry and goes to the kitchen and finishes the remains of a pizza. He washes it down with tepid tap water.

Block checks the voice mail from his phone. "*If you want to find Luna's killer, come to this address.*" Block writes down the address, but memorizes it and forsakes the paper beside his phone as he leaves his home.

Block looks to the moon. A soft breeze scuttles leaves across the driveway. They sound like the scraping of bones.

Block looks at the Crown Vic assigned him by IPD. His Ford pickup truck is parked on the other side. He looks at the sky and with all of his agony wishes to see the moon shine. He is rewarded and shines too, but the moon is quickly covered again by silver clouds.

Block knows that if he chooses the truck he will die.

Block has lived too much, suffered the touch of madmen, tasted the ugly redolence of death and outlived the only human being that ever loved him. Even for a giant, death cultivates life too dear to be abided; death draws final breaths like moths to a light. Death draws even giants.

Block arrives at Mort's warren in his truck. He has a police-issued Glock in his right hand.

The door is open and Block enters. Block takes in the scene before him. He sighs deeply, one of but a few exhalations left him.

Mort is nailed to a cross, a crucifixion in all ways realized. A spear protrudes from his side. A nude young woman lies at his feet, dead. She wears a silk scarf around her diminished neck.

There is candlelight.

Block is not surprised when the man on the cross moves, but is surprised that it is not he that is addressed.

Block hears the man say, "God, have I recompensed?" He watches the man on the cross die, consumed within a shudder, his question answered.

Lystan emerges from the shadows. He holds two sticks, one in each hand. "Old Mort was a fool."

Block sees Lystan as one sees the world as it slips away forever. Block sees in the shadows surrounding Lystan, as appendages, or tumors, a beautiful cow, a dragon and a ram.

Lystan says, "I bring hell with me. You shall see."

Block places a bullet between the eyes of Lystan anyway. *Why not*?

Block's heart spasms and he bends to his knees; and again, Block's heart spasms… He drops face-first upon the floor and before the cross. He pulls arms under him, puts his hands to his chest, as if cupping his essence. Block's heart stops and the giant dies.

Lystan bellows. No one hears his cry.

6.

The giant sees radiance in the distance. He is in a line of people heading toward the light.

Block says, "The line to heaven is a long one."

The man just in front of him tugs at the giant's arm.

Mort says; "At least we're in it."

"You got that right," Abby adds.

Devotion

Sheila Hall

Do you love me?

She repeats the question, over and over in hypnotic overtones. He's on his knees in supplication, mind racing over the tracks of his devotion.

He understands, yet has no clue. The world revolves in known expressions; routines everlasting. But there was nothing before her. Nothing, now that she is here before him. Not even the concrete slicing into his knees warrants acknowledgement. All that is and will ever be is now. The world can drown in its sorrows of loss and regret while his conscience remains pure in the glorious benediction of her presence.

Do you love me?

Every visual detail of her is explored.

He knows in the real world, she is small in stature. But as she stands before him, she is ten feet tall; a lithe and graceful goddess looking down from on high. The benevolent ruler. The soft fabric of her sneakers hide her perfectly painted toenails. Jeans hugging sweetly around all of her contours, a tactile gift for the connoisseur of flesh. Soft fabric cradling her upper body that hides the perfection which is her chest. The slightest hint of nipple shadowing against the harsh overhead lights makes his mouth water.

His gaze settles on her hand. Deceptive, just like the rest of her. A musician's fingers, fluid in motion. Perfectly shaped fingernails adorned with jeweled ruby coloring. These hands would tell a story of privilege through the soft lines of their history. That story would be a lie. She is strong; hands as an extension of her indomitable will, gripping and tearing down reality just to be molded into her image. A utopia realized.

Movement from the corner of his eye and his head is jerked up to confront her, face to face. Water pools in his heavy lids as he looks into the face of heaven. Sharp green eyes stare back and all he can do is cry for one cannot gaze upon the sun and come away unscathed.

Do you love me?

Memories like slides in a projector careen out of control. Bam. The first moment she turned her head in his direction and the world tumbled off its axis. Bam. The first word sounded and all of music stuttered in response then fell away in silence. Bam. Bam. Bam.

Each moment a lifetime of details and discoveries. Each memory a blip among the cosmos.

Do you love me?

He finally answers out loud, sealing the deal. Her gentle smile graces him like the rays of a new day, full of promise and caressing the sodden Earth below. His heart fills to the brim with love and joy. This must be as the birth of creation; infinite possibilities with time stretching in all directions at once.

The flash of light travelling across the edge of steel and the pressure pushing into his chest are the only witnesses of the knife gliding in. The warmth soaking his shirt and jeans mirrors the warmth seeping through his brain. The slowing down of time and energy; a bunny losing its power.

And still she smiles.

His eyes still strain to see her even as his vision slowly fades to black. The endless sleep cradled in her immortal arms. The only thought still holding shape within his mind is: I love you.

The Mysterious Case of the Post-Apocalyptic Oxymoron

Rick Austin

There are many good ways to begin a story.

That wasn't one of them.

I'll never forget that fateful Monday morning. I awoke with a start, looking about my bedroom anxiously. The start turned and looked at me curiously, then relaxed and smiled. I'd picked her up in a bar the night before, it was the typical sort of place where starts would hang out, keen to prey on those who'd hit rock bottom and were looking for a cheap thrill. I hadn't hit rock-bottom yet, but I certainly did like things cheap. I'm a hack, after all.

The sun crept in through the curtains, took a look around, and then crept out. I don't blame it at all. A hack's bedroom is no place to be, not for anybody. Besides, I couldn't afford to have a sun. I was having enough problems making ends meet, and the last thing I needed was a sun hanging around.

"Honey?" the start said, a playful smile making her painted lips curl upwards. It would have been pleasant, if it weren't for the way she reminded me of a shark about to go in for second helpings. "What's wrong? Why don't you go back to sleep?"

I shook my head, no. I couldn't do this, couldn't allow myself to get distracted. I'd been working a case for weeks and had finally wrapped it up. Last night had just been a way to break the monotony. In fact, I hadn't just broken it; I'd shattered it into a million pieces.

"Aw, honey," the start said, full of sympathy. I couldn't tell if it was the genuine article or just a cheap imitation emotion that came with her as a matching set. "You know, last night was wonderful. And you've got nothing to worry about, it happens to all writers at some point."

Dammit, did she have to bring that up *now*? Okay, so I suffer from writer's block sometimes, it's no big deal. Okay, so it's gotten worse over the years, but I guess aging and the day-to-day rigors of life take it out of you after a while. Once your creativity goes, you're out of the game. I know some old guys who don't have any lead left in their pencils, and I just hope I'm never that bad.

I tossed the start a quick glance, and she caught it and put it on. It seemed to fit her pretty well, hugging her curves in all the right places. At least she was a real start and not a false start. I'd woken up with a false start once, and let me tell you that they're not all they're cracked up to be.

"Your story's on the dresser, sweetheart," I told her, playing it cool. Deep down I hated to part with it. It wasn't much, just a couple of pages I'd hastily hacked out overnight, full of plot-holes and bad grammar, but it was still salvageable. It still held some value, and there was at least one decent idea in there. I guess she could get something for it at some pulp printing house, or give it to her john whose name was Gary. I picked up a bottle and poured myself a drink.

She got up, sidled over to the dresser and took it, folding the pages up and slipping them into her handbag. I watched her, and couldn't help but admire her. She was a professional, all right. She had even brought her own protection with her. You know you're dealing with a pro when they bring their own non-disclosure agreements with them, and she'd made me sign it before I'd written a single damn word.

"What do you know about the Post-Apocalyptic Oxymoron?"

Her question took me by surprise. It was something everyone in the game knew about, but that we just didn't talk about. It was the world's biggest open secret. It was always in the thoughts of every writer, from the worst Hollywood hacks to the most cultured novelists who live like recluses and wear smoking jackets behind their high walls. I stared at her, unsure of how much to say.

"It's just a myth," I replied, not wanting to tip my hand because if I did then I'd spill my drink. "It's a fairy tale. And I'm no fairy, despite my underwear being a little frilly around the edges."

"It's no fairy tale," the start said. She looked at me in a way that made my pulse race and break the world record, before doing a victory lap with its arms raised in triumph. "I've heard that the Post-Apocalyptic Oxymoron arrived in town on the 5 o'clock train yesterday, the one that arrived at quarter past six."

"Bull," I spat out with disbelief.

She looked at the bull, now lying on the floor in a small pile of spittle. She eyed it with distaste. Wasn't that just typical of a vegan?

"I'm serious," she continued. "Some of the girls at the bar were talking about it. One of them is the sister of Arms Akimbo, the henchman. He used to run with the Scissors mob, until it got too dangerous. He told his sister that the Oxymoron was hitting town to make a big score, and there's not a writer out there who would take the chance of taking him on."

Take a chance. That was the problem. No hack out there ever took chances; they always preferred the community chest. But if the information was true, this could be my time to pass go, collect the two hundred bucks and maybe even get some free parking.

"What else do you know?" I asked. If I was going to pursue this I would have to be prepared like a Boy Scout. "And more importantly, why are you telling me this?"

"I'm telling you this because I think you can do it. You're good. Better than most, anyway. I heard that the Post-Apocalyptic Oxymoron is going to be staying at the Shillton hotel."

"The Shillton? I thought that place closed down years ago," I replied. "It kept crumbling under pressure. It kept letting too many in and couldn't take it."

"That's the one," she said with a nod. "But they've reopened it. I guess it was someone's dream project. It's good to have goals, and the Shillton's a great place to start if you've got some of your own."

I gathered my thoughts up and stuffed them in a plastic bag, even though I could have sworn I'd asked for paper. If the Oxymoron was in town, it meant trouble. The only reason why nobody would touch him was because all those other people who put ink on paper... well, they had common sense. If I'd had any, I'd have known that I was getting in too deep and three was a crowd. One of us had to go.

"Thanks for the information, sweetheart," I said with a slight grin, "but it's time you hit the trail. Thanks for the inspiration, though."

With a sly smile, she slipped her purse over her shoulder and started to leave. She turned back to me and said, "You're going after him, aren't you? The Oxymoron."

"Damn, skippy," I replied, and gave her a wink. To this day I don't know what she did with it.

***

I took a cab to the Shillton Hotel, which was weird because normally the taxis take *me*.

It's the donkey, the carrot and the stick thing, you know how it goes. Between me, the taxi and my wallet, we had to argue amongst ourselves about which one got to be what. I didn't mind being stuck with the stick, and I figured that the cab should have been the donkey because it was fun to ride on and the driver was acting like an ass. It beat trying to ride on the carrot, even if some people tend to like that sort of thing.

Looking around the city, I couldn't help but think of how it had changed since Christmas. It had been a magical time of year, even if Mother Nature had pulled the town's pants down and dumped a big pile of snow inside its underwear. When the New Year balls had dropped, the snow had melted into a slushy ooze and poured into the gutters like a sloppy trickle down a trouser leg. The stain it had left at the time had been awful, and the mayor had tried to pass it off as something else. But the locals knew better.

When Spring had sprung, it had brought a renewed sense of life to things here. The city had become a place where the flowers were in bloom and the sundresses never set. It looked magical, and it proved that Mother Nature and Father Time could have some great kids when they weren't arguing about which one of them forgot to get the birth control.

We pulled up outside the Shillton, and then put it down again. It was an old brownstone that had been painted a golden shade of black. Well, you know how these rich people can be when it comes to taste. They usually don't have much of it, and the little they do possess is questionable and struggles to find the answers.

They wouldn't know real class if they had attended it for three semesters and were given crib sheets.

I paid the cab driver a couple of bills, and he complained that he wanted either Bobs or Georges. Some people are never happy. I learned that a long time ago, back when I was married. My ex-wife wanted the Bobs and Georges too, and had them by the boatload. I'm a pretty liberal-minded guy, or at least a liberal-minded guy who's pretty, but even I couldn't put up with that kind of behavior. It taught me a harsh lesson, and I was just passing it on to the cabbie. Pay it forward, that's the trick.

I entered the Shillton and it was the sort of place where hopes and dreams could be had for fifty dollars a night, or for a hundred if you wanted clean sheets and a sandwich from room service.

The lobby lived up to its name, and I approached the main desk. The man behind it looked like the reception clerk that time forgot. I gave him a cool stare, maybe seventy degrees if I got my angle and temperature right.

"I hear that there's a big shot staying here," I said with casual cool. "Some kind of... Oxymoron."

The clerk, whose nametag read "Kent," gasped in surprise. I suppose he wasn't used to such indirectly direct questions. "There... well, there *is* an Oxymoron staying here. Although I really can't divulge any more information than that, sir."

He'd already given me more than enough to go on, but I couldn't resist needling him like an old sock. "Darn it,' I said. "This isn't some kind of social visit. It's a matter of life and death. Probably mine and yours. Now which one of us gets to hold the lily?"

Kent gulped, and I could see that my lightly veiled threat was doing the dance where seven of them came off on the quick. "The Oxymoron... the Oxymoron's up on ninth, in 711. You can take the elevator."

I thanked him and tipped him generously. He regained his balance and gave me a nervous look. I didn't know if he was worried for me or himself, but I knew which way I'd have bet. Well, I was the one doing the tough job and it would have to be on me.

The elevator was one of those old-fashioned kinds that went both up *and* down. It creaked a little as I took it up to the ninth, and when I got there I was floored. They had security up the wazoo, which was a weird place to have it if you weren't into the kinky stuff.

There was a real gorilla guarding the door to 711, and a couple of trained apes who were backing him up. Normally, I would treat these guys as a joke and make some quip about how the whole situation was bananas, but I couldn't monkey around. I had to be careful and not act prematurely.

I acted like I belonged there, walking up to 710 with all the confidence of a podiatrist sauntering up to a new pair of orthopedic loafers. The apes studied me for a moment, and I pulled a set of keys from my pocket casually. I dropped them on purpose, and the apes loped over to help. Before they knew it, I was delivering express uppercuts to them and had them paying C.O.D. They slumped to the floor before the gorilla guarding 711 could even react.

They say that the element of surprise is half the battle and number eight in the periodic table. I'm no scientist, I'm a *writer*; for me, my surprises come with an added twist. The gorilla was slow and clumsy, all muscle and no brainpower. He was still going for his gun when I gave him the bum's rush, and as bums went, this one was particularly smelly.

He collapsed in a heap that the cleaner had left there earlier, and I picked up his gun. I don't usually carry one, it's not my style, but I was in way over my head and I knew it. I turned it over in my hands, and saw that the gorilla must have been the possessive type because he'd scrawled his name over it. In white painted letters it had the name *TOMMY* going down it. Tommy's gun was nice, and I figured that if nothing else, it would make a good souvenir.

"Who's better, who's best?" I asked Tommy as I turned to face the room he had been guarding.

I kicked in the door to 711, charging into the room like a scribbler possessed. I knew that at this point it was all or nothing. I'd gone too far now, and if I tried to back out then I'd go crashing into some garbage cans and would have to pay the insurance.

And there it was.

The Post-Apocalyptic Oxymoron, large as life and certainly a whole lot prettier.

It was resting on a long, wooden table, a golden glow emanating from it, powered by pure creativity. I couldn't stop staring at it, and barely noticed the man seated next to it.

"I've been expecting you," the man said. I focused on him, and couldn't believe my eyes. It was Reginald Ulation, my old writing partner.

I hadn't seen him since he'd skipped out of town, hopping up and down as he stole the script we'd been working on together. It was only afterwards that I'd found out he had a history of conning people out of their work, plagiarizing it, then hiring others to rewrite it and finally plagiarizing the work that had already been plagiarized. He was a story-launderer, and at the time, I'd been suckered in like an amateur vacuum salesman.

"It's been a while, Reg," I said with a cold sneer. "What's it been? Two years? Two too few."

"It's been a couple, sure," he replied with a smirk. "I see you've still got a way with words."

"Better than getting away with words," I commented.

"Touché," he said, and paused. If either of us in the room was a touché, it was definitely him. He gestured to the Oxymoron. "It's magnificent, isn't it? I imagine that you're curious how I came to acquire it."

I glared at him. "Not particularly," I said, cutting off a needlessly long-winded backstory. If there's one thing I hate, it's exposition. "All I care about is that you have it… and I want it."

"I can understand that. It's what all writers crave, what they search for their entire lives. They obsess over it, addicted just to the mere thought of it. It corrupts the soul of every writer who dreams of it, and I own it. What makes you think that I'd ever part with it, and what makes you think you're worthy?"

I hesitated, considering his questions. I stared at Tommy's gun, heavy in my hands, knowing that I could fill him with more lead than an HB pencil. This was no surprise, since lead pencils don't contain actual lead but graphite. That's just in case you were interested. It's trivia like that which makes stories fun. But the gun, it was a tempting thought.

The tension filled the room. He wanted answers, and they had to be good.

"I'll give you fifty bucks for it," I said.

"Okay," he said with a shrug. "Do you need a bag to carry it in?"

"Paper, if you've got one. Plastic if it's all you've got."

And, like that, the deal was done. I walked out of his room, a fifty down but in possession of the greatest literary device known to man, the ultimate weapon in the war of words. And I know how to wield it properly.

Even though I never saw him again, I still remember the question that Reg had asked me. He had wanted to know what made me worthy of possessing it, when other writers had tried and failed so many times. I didn't tell him, but I know the answer and it's the same one I tell everyone:

"I'm not just any writer; I'm a hack."

And I'm damn proud of being one…

Confession and Redemption of the Apostle Abbot Technobabble

Michael Allen Rose

You want me to explain about the butterflies? Okay. My name's Abbot. But everyone calls me Technobabble. I'm a prophet.

I'm a Lou Reed-level mystery. An equation wrung from imaginary numbers. A shaved dog in winter. A vessel full of helium and all the ignorance in the book of knowin'. What? Yeah, *Transformer* WAS a good album. Look, you wanna hear the truth or talk music criticism? Okay then. I grew up believin' morality was concrete, insoluble and inscrutable, and everyone had ta' pick a side. Believed in God and the Devil and all them saints. There were the things of the angels, cloudy and transparent, endless harp music and napalm that made you burn like a stick of innocence. Then, there were things darker, complex and throbbing, poetry in motion but the motion is a burnin' page in a book of kindling. I usedta' call out in the dark to slithering, crawling things, silence speaking volumes an' calling out lyrics to death metal diatribes, tryin' to get some treasure out of the chest we call life. Turned out, it was a one-sided phone conversation. I dropped in the quarter, but the demons never returned my change.

Turns out, I was prayin' in the wrong direction.

"As the meatball caps the mountain peak, our aspirations doth flow upward to his noodley appendages from whence all blessings and various sauces flow."
(Writings of Ziti the Baked 5:2, Apocryphal).

Then, everything changed. I was in the park, beggin' for quarters and lookin' the brooding part; hair hangin' in my face like vines creepin' across a cracked tombstone. Drug circles under my eyes, hammocks for dull, clouded corneas glazed over like doughnuts. Believed in and rejected everything and nothin'. All my heavy metal records taught me that praying to the devil involved guitars and leather pants, and I didn't have a dollar to buy either. I'm sittin' there in a dirty wife-beater without the wife, croonin' about the rough life I got it when suddenly, I smell spicy Italian cooking. I try to take a bite of the air, and smack my teeth together.

"Lo, I shall come to you wafting on the breeze, for I am everywhere you want to be, as with a credit card. Seek me out with all senses, and deliciousness shall be your reward." (Parmesean 12:3-4).

A gentleman strolls by. I can tell he's a gentleman 'cuz his hat is clean and his fingernails are trimmed. He's eatin' with a plastic fork out a styrofoam box, and I stretch my neck up like a periscope breaking the surface of a tar pit. He spins his fork and wraps up a nest of noodles, the world's largest roadside ball of twine right there on the end of his stabbin' stick. He shovels the mass into his maw and masticates, dribbles of tomato blood trickling over his bottom lip and nestling into the wispy hairs he calls a beard.

He looks at me and says, "Yeah?"

I look right back and say, "Change?"

His face gets all lemony as he pats his pocket and shrugs; he does something unexpected. He hands me the box of spaghetti.

"Want this?" he says.

Nothing is what I say, but I take his refuse and chow down, gorging myself on lukewarm pasta and savin' the meatball for the coup de gracie. I look up to thank the guy, but he's already turned into a bush and there's nothin' but green around me, so I go back to my lunch.

"In times of woe and sorrow, my meatballs shall sustain you, in times of sadness, my starches shall flood your belly with life, in times of change, my noodley appendages shall tickle your brain and you shall lapse into a food coma of great perseverance." (Song of Alfredo 5:1).

Getting back to the meatball, I scan it for teeth marks. It's clean, so I dive in, stabbing it through the North Pole and spinnin' it toward the black hole of my mouth. I feel a beam of light penetrate my skull as the meatball goes supernova. An explosion of juicy wonderment echoes off my teeth and gums, reverberates up through my eustachian tubes and careens off each eardrum like a pinball. I wanna' scream, but my throat muscles are shredded wheat. I wanna' run, but my feet are frozen in blocks of dry ice. I'm very hungry.

A voice in my head asks, "Is there a God?"

I reply, "Does it matter?"

The voice says, "Where do we go when we die?"

I say, "Detroit."

The voice says, "What dictates morality?"

I say, "The price of spaghetti sauce in Florence."

Then I see it: the fabled city on a hill in my mind's eye, the prophet atop the mountain. It is the largest plate of spaghetti and meatballs I have ever seen, stretching up to blot out the horizon.

"My house has many chambers, and in those many chambers many doors. Behind each door is a room filled with a nice spicy arribiata with basil, and all those who climb to the summit shall live with me in my noodley mansion for eternity." (1st Pesto 3:1-2).

No, I ain't digressin', I'm just sayin'! The butterflies haven't shown up yet. Right now, they're an unknown factor. That part's comin'; you gotta be patient. So. I know I'm supposed to climb the mountain, but it's way high and kind of scary. Cannon-fire explodes from somewhere in the distance. Then I see it comin' over the edge of the world, all fire and hailstones, a tall ship, masts spiking the sky with pinpricks. Aboard, a happy crew of sailors dance around.

"What ho, landlubber?" a stocky man with an eye-patch and a parrot calls out.

"What ho, indeed!" I reply.

"Where be your eye-patch?" he screams.

"I don't need one!" I yell into the wind.

Out of nowhere, a wrapped piece of hard candy hits my eye. I feel some blood vessels break and the world swims. Before I can react, lines are dropping from the side of the vessel, hooks are underneath my arms, and I'm hauled over the side onto knotty wooden boards, polished to a shine. Someone fits an eye-patch on me, and I feel the urge to yo-ho-ho.

"Thou shalt find ye a merry band of marauders, for they shalt lift ye up when thou art crabby, and share your rum when your barrels overflow." (Beardy the Foul 3:1).

I found myself wonderin' where our destination was, but that was all soon forgotten once the wenches showed up. In between swabbin' decks and shinin' cannonballs, we sang piratey songs and frolicked with wenches. Up the mountain we sailed, over the vast waves of noodles, off-white, al dente peaks and valleys tappin' out the rhythms of otherworldly songs beneath our trailin' sails. I'm danglin' my legs off the side of the ship, and some scurvy dog creaks his way over and plops down beside me. He's the wreck of the ancient mariner. A lighthouse gone dark. His knees pop like firecrackers as he folds himself into a sittin' position.

"Heard the good news, boy?" he croaks.

"Don't believe in good news." said I, with a punk-rock sneer bred of ill-tempered angst.

"Stand up," he says.

Not havin' a reason to argue, I do, but I don't at the same time. My legs stretch upward, and carry my torso northbound as my vertebrae stack one-by-one atop each other, but for some reason, my gaze stays on the level. We're lookin' each other in the eye-patch, and I press down leg-wise to get taller. But, despite my best efforts, I'm shrunk like a wiener in a swimmin' pool.

"What's goin' on?" I scream.

The mummy in front of me just laughs and shrugs. "You feel it, then? That's his noodley appendage, pressing down on you. He's showing you how much he loves you."

I could tell by lookin' there weren't enough squirrels in this guy's school-bus. Shoulda' hit him with a side of beef-fried logic, but as I stood there, I felt squeaks in my spine. His noodley appendage descended from the ceiling-sky, throwin' the theory of gravity out the window and pressin' his starchy love bone-deep. The pirates began to sing sea shanties, yo-ho-hoing up a storm, as I was filled with understanding. All the theories I'd heard growin' up, the things I'd missed in school because I was too high to pay attention, the brain cells killed by experiments in self-trepanation… those fistulas and holes in my sclera didn't matter because the Flying Spaghetti Monster was watchin' over me with an aura of soft but firm love.

"His love is endless, like the servings of bread-sticks and salad at Olive Garden." (Writings of Brother Thistle, Monastic Dynasty of Asiago, circa 1643, Apocryphal).

A huge crash split the silence and I was thrown off my feet into the railing. The pirates shouted: "Shinobi!" I turned just in time to see a group of ninjas doing a series of flips onto the poop deck, over-elaborate multi-handled pokin' sticks flailin' around them like electric pulses. A pair of rail-thin ninjas leaped head over heels at me, and I fell backward just in time to avoid a couple of punctured lungs and some muscle turned to hamburger. I hit the ground and saw the old man standing over me, his face a torn up newspaper with ugly headlines. He handed me a cutlass. Now, this was sweet! I hoped I wasn't too late to turn the tide, but I sat up too fast and got me a head-rush.

"Many ninjas did come from the hills and the forests surrounding them, and the lamentations were great. Yo-ho-ho, they cried, this be our last day!" (Piraticus 32:5).

A katana blade sliced the air next to my head as I rolled sideways. Eh? How do I know it was a katana blade? I ain't ignorant. I've seen every ninja movie ever made. Yes, that even includes *The Thundering Ninja*, where the man jogs down the street holdin' one-pound weights in each hand and *Clash of the Ninjas* where the bad-guy ninja holds the phone three inches away from his head while talking. I didn't say I was a ninja, I said I was a prophet. Listen: My eyes met those of a ninja assassin as I lifted my cutlass to guard against his second blow. As our swords clashed, sparks blasted my eyebrows off my face. I felt these little hairs rainin' down across my nose, like tiny cooked pieces of fusilli and it lit a fire inside my guts. I was a pot-belly stove filled with gasoline and lightnin'. Acid bubbled up from my stomach like a thunder peal. I was a chargin' bull, a fallin' piano made of pain and magic, a thumb-wrestlin' champ at a hitch-hiking competition. I stood like a redwood, seeds of rage spreadin' from me in a cloud and I brought my cutlass down, slicing the ninja in half. He deflated like a wrinkled suit. A blanket made of ninja covering several lumps, movin' around like a bag of maggots. My hands work fast, findin' the edge of the ninja and I whip it up like a parachute revealing a slew of pissed-off penguins.

"The cold eyes of the flightless bore into us. We feared we would be lost, but for our flying, noodley lord. We fell upon our knees in supplication and lo, his noodley appendage did come to save us from their squawking beaks, their beating flippery wings and their dapper fashion sense." (The Earth-Shattering Epiphanies of Earl 30:10-12).

They squawk at me, a gaggle of car alarms, flappin' furious. I squawk back, but when I look up, there's no longer a boat, no longer a sea, no pirates and no ninjas. Instead, a furious snowstorm is blowin' up. I watch the penguins blow away. Right about now, I'm feelin' pretty confused, and angry, see? My tender brain has been chopped up like coke on a toilet tank. So that's when I start rantin' and ravin', swingin' my sword; a Bruce Lee movie with Michael Bay explosions. More and more penguins are flying by. Fuck that! Penguins aren't supposed to fly, so I cut them down with my terrible sword! I was just defending myself and my pirate brethren, you see? It was a clear cut case of religious intolerance! Anyway, the maelstrom of squawks and thunder and crashing blades takes shape, and this voice blasts across my eardrums. "Arrrgh!"

"In the beginning was the word, and the word was 'Arrrgh.'" (Piraticus 13:7).

Beside the point? The verses aren't beside the point, they ARE the point. They have everything do with the butterflies. They're gospel, holy writ, volumes of the sacred law, recipes for al-dente salvation. The voice was that of He, Him, It, His Holy Noodley-ness, none other than our starchy Lord and Flavour, the Flying Spaghetti Monster. He didn't speak English. My ears felt damp. Filled with cotton soaked in crude oil. Underwater love straight to my brain-pan. I just knew the visions he was sendin' me were the truest truth there could be. Penguins were midgets who scorned him, you know, and they are damned for eternity to the cold wastes of Antarctica. Unholy abominations. But what to do? Surely, our noodley creator has endless love for his creations, and wouldn't use his appendages to destroy even beasts so foul as them who'd lost his favor. I thought about this long and hard as I rode one of his glistening noodles down at the speed of meat, descendin', plummeting toward the plate of Earth like a ripe plum tomato. He gently placed me right where I'd started my journey, but I'd changed. This time, there wouldn't be no beggin' and no dopin', just pure good, old-time religion. He had given me a holy task. I was a crusader, a headless John, no martyr I, but instead of a force of noodley vengeance.

"His wrath is great, but his love is boundless." That's one of mine. It's new.
(Book of me. Technobabble Alpha:1).

So I've been ponderin' this irksome issue for eons, when suddenly it hits me. Chaos theory. Just like gravity and friction, the Flying Spaghetti Monster set things into motion and gave us the hammers and nails to move mountains and valleys. With the weather patterns changin' it makes super-sense. Apocalypse-level fires in Arizona, land-drownin', floodin' in North Dakota, tornadoes bigger than the world's largest ball of twine in Oklahoma. It takes one spark off an ancient redwood matchstick, choked on gasoline to light the spark that will wash those penguins right out of the Lord's hair. Well, it ain't actually hair, it's spaghetti, but you surf my driftwood. Anyway, the butterfly effect. If one of them flaps the right wing you get rains of frogs. Flocks of birds frozen in ice. Earth rupturing like a popped pimple. Fire fallin' from the clouds. So if a whole bunch of them were to set themselves flappin' to the beat of my drum, we could change the world.

Antarctica would wash right off the planet and become just another ice sculpture floatin' through space.

Obviously, what I've been doin' wasn't vandalizin', it was EVANGELIZING. I have a zoo pass, I got a right ta be here. So I was freein' all the butterflies in the nature building to create a mighty flap. The wind of a god-fart. Right here! Consequences bein' what they are, cause and effect affectin' physical reality and realistic physics as we know them, the chaos is gonna build up. Mercury in a thermometer, until that water is just boilin', and kapow! The underpants of the world go shootin' off into the void. We're finally gonna be free! The pirates can come back! Global warming will cease! The whole place will just be better off. Earth is gonna be a rent-controlled apartment with free cable from now on!

Don't talk to me about how expensive them butterflies are. Can't put a price on changin' the world! This is big. Moses built the pyramids big. Abraham fightin' off the giant whale big. Jesus turnin' people into pigs big. This will make all that look like crappy street magic on a three-card monte table. Disorderly what? Sir, I conduct myself as a philosopher does, an anarchist in sheep's clothing. I can't disturb the peace if there isn't any! And I certainly didn't steal anythin'. If you love somethin', let it go and murder blasphemous penguins!

Yes officer, I'll come quietly. But I ain't removin' the strainer.

The Splash

Andy de Fonseca

Alan Jason Robert-Allen was a simple man. He woke up via alarm clock, was scared to put his feet on the cold floor, tied his tie, drank his shitty coffee, and took the train to work. It doesn't matter what he did, because he didn't care enough himself. He did it because it was the thing to do; it got him to the weekend, to the beer with his friends, the vomit at 2 a.m., and on good nights, the broad in the cheap heels. His age was starting to pass him by, but not quite enough where he needed to worry. His looks were still there but waning, more due to the lack of ambition than age. His home was also simple, but home. He went out of the country once, but Canada could hardly be called an accomplishment.

On one particular morning, after he finished his bland coffee and store-brand fruit rings, Alan stood pressed against the door on the cramped train, forced to look out and see the world. The bright morning light reflected off the passing windows and shot into his eyes as though there were a machine gun firing rays of sun. He soon got a headache, but with someone else's balls pressed against his butt cheeks, there wasn't much he could do; even when he closed his eyes, the flashing light was there. So he stared, burned his retinas, and caught the beautiful woman dressing in front of her window as if she were deaf and blind to the loud public transportation that careened by just twenty feet away.

That would have been an immediate boner if it weren't for his junk being squashed against the cold metal door.

That day at work, Alan sat at his desk unable to concentrate on whatever the fuck it was he did. There were charts in front of him? A webinar that needed to be set up? Some emails needed to be answered. But the light, teal bra with mismatched panties flashed in front of him. A single bullet in the barrel of the gun had caught him right between the eyes. It wasn't even a case of easy arousal that kept him from his work, but the interruption from his normal, habitual life. It was that splash of teal on the grey canvas that stretched from his eighth birthday up to at least the strip club he'd be inhabiting this Friday from 11 p.m. to 5 a.m. It had awoken the reality of his sad, pathetic situation, so much so, that he ran to the bathroom to vomit.

As Alan Jason Robert-Allen bowed before the porcelain goddess and emptied the weak coffee and stale fruit rings into the crisp, white bowl routinely maintained by the skyscraper's cleaning crew, his coworkers came and went. Some stopped out of genuine concern, some stopped to save face. Once finished, Alan decided to do his morning constitutional, to save him the walk back and forth between bathroom and cubical. It was usually a fifteen minute affair, complete with games on his phone and reading his dailies. Today, all he thought of was the splash of teal.

Today, it took longer.

Finally, with a gentle push, he felt the release and the loss of a couple pounds.

"OPAAAAAAAA!!!!"

Jumping through a stall door was never a plan in the fight-or-flight response, but Alan had never expected to make the decision while sitting on the throne. He landed outside the stall, pants down, flaccid penis out, eyes bulging. A couple of gentlemen in suits, dicks in hands, turned from their urinals and stared. Alan stared back, wondering why *they* were giving *him* the raised eyebrow. After several long moments, long after eye contact should have ended, realizing he still had to wipe, Alan scooted back into the stall; pretty sure he left a trail on the floor behind him.

He quietly shut the door and peered under the stall next to him. Nothing. Nothing for the next ten stalls to the wall on the end. He looked into his bowl. Yesterday's conception and today's pride and joy looked back. He flushed it down and left.

That evening on the way home, Alan stood like a stone in front of the train doors in order to have a view of the window that opened his eyes to a new color in the world. Passengers called him a prick when he wouldn't move, but it didn't matter to him. They didn't know. Their worlds were not yet bathed in the pure light of teal blue, and therefore they did not know this window view was worth fighting for.

As the sun silhouetted the building, a clear view into the room was easy. At least, it would have been if there were any lights on. But it was dark. And the battle was lost. Alan couldn't figure out why he felt so anxious on his walk home. He recalled the flash of beauty over and over in his head. The remaining figment of this unexpected, yet long awaited dream was being hushed out by constant replay, growing fuzzier with each reimagination. He tried to grasp onto it, cling to every detail, yet now, he was beginning to wonder if it was all a fantasy on his bored morning commute.

That evening, relaxed on the toilet and waiting for biology to take its course, Alan didn't come anywhere near his high score on his phone game. When he finally felt it drop-

"OPAAAAAAAA!!!!!"

This time Alan shouted a profanity and even got annoyed. Maybe once he could have imagined something like this, but twice? It was that splash of teal. That's what it was. He quickly sat back on the toilet and forced out whatever else he could. There was a small drop in the water.

"OPAAAAAAAA!!!!"

He ran out of the bathroom, slipped on the pants around his ankles, and hit his head on the floor. Alan didn't wake up until noon the next day. He showered his ass, flushed the toilet from the night before, and ran to the train, skipping his flavorless coffee and sugar rings. On the train, Alan concluded he was going crazy, and these were his final days of sanity. Yet instead of fulfilling goals and living his dreams, all he wanted to do was sit back and watch the end of his world. That was, until he saw the window open and a fluid arm welcome in the spring breeze. The teal bra was draped over a chair near the window, not as respectfully as he would have liked for something that had awoken a new meaning of life in him.

Not having eaten for half a day, but instead being unconscious face-down on the floor all evening and morning, Alan stopped by the first food truck he found and ordered whatever the lady before him requested. The happy man in the traveling kitchen handed him a styrofoam container, money was swapped, and Alan went on his way. Inside the container, he was greeted with a large meatball on a steaming pile of noodly heaven. Shoving it in his mouth was pure delight until a homeless man popped up from the bushes.

Alan swallowed. "Yeah?"

The homeless man looked back. "Change?"

Usually Alan would have kept walking, but the look in the man's eyes was one of yearning, one of searching. One that had seen the teal in the world, and lost it. Alan patted his pockets and recalled the last of his bills going over the counter in The Great Spaghetti Exchange of Five Minutes Ago. He looked back at the homeless man, those eyes despondent and defeated, but wiser than most. Alan handed over the styrofoam box.

"Want this?" he asks.

As the man chowed down, Alan turned to leave, and immediately fell, hurting his knee badly. The rest of the work day went just as well.

Blaming the spaghetti, Alan was ready to burst that night when he returned home from his nameless job at whatever company on FuckItAll Street. With his pants to the floor, he forwent the phone games and instead, stared straight ahead at the pale yellow of the bathroom wall. He was unsure if his thirst for teal was a genuine passion or a fleeting moment of lust; he was sure, however, that it wasn't about love, but a lack thereof. A lack of many things he thought his life would be at one time, years ago. A lack of certainty, contentment. A lack of knowing who he was or who he wanted to be. A lack-

"OPAAAAAAAA!!!"

Alan banged his fist on the wall. Over and over again he banged his fucking fist on the fucking wall because this fucking yelling. All he fucking wanted was to shit in peace but now there's a whole stadium cheering him on every time he let one drop. What in all seven made-up hells was going on!

Alan sighed, wiped, pulled up his pants, flushed the toilet, and went to bed.

The days pass, with each day Alan hoping for a peek into the life of teal from his nut-crushing, ball-to-ass rubbing spot on the train. Sometimes, he got to see a breath of the soft blue, and sometimes, even new colors. But each time, he knew, was never as good as the first. And each time, instead, as the months passed, it was a constant reminder of all his world was without. For how long would he have this quiet affair from afar? For how long would he let this lingerie control every ounce of him? It was everything he wanted, yet he dared not knock on the door and request more. That teal consumed him, controlled him, was everything to him. It was defeating him.

"OPAAAAAAAA!!!!"

Alan zipped up and went to wash his hands.

"They were quieter today," Brian from marketing smiled politely. "Been stressed?"

Alan shrugged and lathered up. Truth was, they had been getting quieter for weeks. Instead of an entire stadium celebrating his rectal evacuations, complete with vuvuzela, half the fans had left, or simply sat down. Alan even went for a prostate exam but the proctologist was clueless as to why the shouts were dimming, as Alan checked out just fine, clear of any cancers.

In Alan's fleeting moment of sight from the train, the window revealed boxes stacked in the empty room. Instead of color there were grey walls and brown cardboard.

That night, there was no 'opa'.

After that night, there were none at all.

The grey canvas of his life continued with its usual ashen hue through the years, and despite those few splatters of color from that brief period in his life, every time he sat, he was looking for a shout of praise. He eyes stopped glancing up when he passed the window, and he eventually buried himself in the middle of the train car, to be as far as he could from the memories. The sunlight reflecting off the windows was now an annoyance and he turned away to block it out.

Alan Jason Robert-Allen was uncomfortable on the starch-white sheets with the fluorescent lighting constantly hovering over him. He was often uncomfortable these days. He wanted to be home, in his simple home, but doctor's orders. Instead, he watched the same shitty show, ate the same shitty oatmeal paste, and slept when they told him to sleep. Dying wasn't all that bad; he never expected to go out with a bang, anyway. The nurses always left the blinds open, so the bright morning sun reflecting off the buildings across the street always woke him, promising him another day, but only reminding him of what he had always hoped to forget.

Today, the tubes connected to his arm seemed to be doing little. The aches in his joints seemed to fade with each breath, and each breath he took seemed to dissolve into a wheezed pant. A single nurse stood by his bed, once a young beauty now turned an older jewel with no evanescent end to her gracefully aged looks. On her lapel, a teal carnation was pinned, and from this carnation a burst of life. A burst of all he wished he had, all he wished he had done, all he wished he had been. A burst of regret. A burst of thanks and overwhelming joy for those few specks of color on an otherwise monotonous canvas.

The fierce sting of fluorescents faded, and soon the outlines of the windows across the street. All that was left was the golden beauty and her splash of teal. Soon, she, too, was gone, but the teal remained. It remained as all went dark, and remained when he had no strength to inhale again. The teal was there as every sound hushed and he was left with nothing but thoughts. The flash of color, of life, remained as everything relaxed, and all was nothing but that soft, pale blue. And in the distance, he heard the stadium, cheering him on. They stamped their feet and grew to a roar, welcoming him back, greeting him as though he had never left, and was always the person he had always hoped he could be, that time when he first saw the color of the world. His body slipped away, and he slipped into the teal ovation.

"OPAAAAAAAA!!!"

Fartday the 13th

M.C. O'Neill

For Leza Cantoral

"And so, then I said, 'While you in there satisfying that old bag all night, I was out on the porch eating hot, buttered corn! Haw-haw!'"

"Oh, God!" Ethan slapped a double face-palm. "That was the stupidest story ever. I think I just lost twenty I.Q. points."

Mason threw his hands in the air. "Hey, what can I say? At least it had a good twist to it."

-Friday, October 13th 2023-

Crackling flames from the campfire flashed the instant Mason spat a full jigger of Bacardi 151 into its burning bowels. The blast startled all present despite their slowed reflexes from heads full of weed and liquor. Dry winds coming in from the dying trees only helped to fan the embers ever higher.

"Hey!" the fraternity brother announced. "I've got a great idea."

Sophia rolled her eyes. "Not another tale of one of your supposed country-time sexual conquests?"

Mason stood up from the rickety lawn chair, stumbled a bit. "Nah, nah. Nothing like that. See, I've been eating on this big ol' can of beans all night…"

He thrust the can of the noxious-smelling, pre-processed food in the young co-ed's face for effect. Its label read in blaring typography, "Mean Beans – Chunky Weens." To that, she crossed her eyes and pinched her nostrils while sucking on her blue raspberry marijuana popsicle.

Ignoring her rebuff, Mason pivoted away toward Ethan. "All right. My idea is this: I'm gonna have Pussyboy Wetballs over here hold out his popsicle. Just a bit beyond the flames."

With blue-stained lips, Sophia groaned, "Oh, shit. I think I know where this is going…"

A look of flickering apprehension washed over Ethan's face. The lime-green popsicle wobbled in his hand as his nerves began to amp. "What the fuck?"

"Lissen," Mason slurred. "It'll be fun. I got a hell of a bad bitch brewing up in me and I never am one to let a good crisis go to waste. So, what I'm gonna do is drop trou while you hold the popsicle behind the fire like I just said. Then, I'm going to let loose with all my ass's might and melt that fucker in one booming blow!"

Ethan whooped at his broheimer's asinine plan. "Ha! Okay! Let's do it!"

The alpha male met his subordinate's mirth. He grabbed the seam of his crotch and pumped it twice at his face with pride. "Hell, yeah! Chunky ween..."

Mason turned around and made good on his promise as he slid his *Fubu Retros* down to his ankles, thus exposing the angry zit on his left butt cheek. In typical douchebag style, he turned his White Sox ballcap backward and braced his hands on his knees. It was now the time of reckoning.

There was no smell. The blaze of the campfire, the growing winds and the sheer immediacy of the ludicrous stunt quelled that foul sensation for the trio. A blue monsoon of flapping anal gas rushed through the tiny pyre that would soon grow to devour the near-decrepit city of Chicago, Illinois.

The brain-addled jock's plan worked well – too well. Ethan's popsicle was vaporized in half of an instant into nothing more than a chartreuse cloud. Soon after, screams of pain and shock ensued.

"AIIEE! My hand!" Ethan wilhelmed as the fire rode up the sleeve of his woolen baja. His fist had become nothing more than the head of a fleshy torch.

"Your hand?" Mason screeched. "What about my *ass*?"

It was all much too funny. Perhaps it was due to the dope, but Sophia thrust out her arms and pointed at each flaming frat boy while cackling away like a wicked witch.

When poor Mason had flatulated, little did he realize that there was a slight possibility that an air pocket in his guts could suck the methane content of the fart back into his colon. Under normal circumstances, the guy was a pretty lucky fellow. He had no problem with the ladies, was born to a wealthy, albeit corrupt, Chicago alderman and usually got whatever new gadget hit the market whenever he wanted it. On that fateful night, good luck was not on the menu for the poor dipshit.

A stiff, October gust blew the scorching streak right up the fart's jetstream like a wick on a bundle of dynamite. As fast as the gas had expelled, its trail rocketed in between his cheeks. In that instant, a large reserve of volatile effluvium still wafting inside of his body combusted with all the anger of the hells. Thusly, his ass exploded.

She couldn't help it. Sophia continued to guffaw.

"Stop laughing, you bitch!" Mason cried. "My asshole's on fire!"

As Ethan ran in one direction, Mason waddled, jeans around ankles, off in the other on their hopeless quests for lovely water. It looked like his posterior was the rear end of a nitrous-fueled drag racer from the 1970's. Instead of glutes, only burning meat and blackened gristle existed where once a butthole nestled.

Looming thickets of the gloomy nature preserve, dry as ever in the autumn night, beckoned Mason as he was in the throes of fiery panic. Ethan made better ground as he still had his pants on. In either direction, a parched forest awaited to be set alight.

Light it did. Each of the brothers of Iaeta Smegma Pi were fully immolated the second they made contact with the thirsty trees. They were both the sparks to a much grander fire that would soon bloom into Hell on Earth.

Due to the preceding summertime drought, the forest was so much rice paper. The chaotic winds blew through the blaze, only to feed it with more precious oxygen. Ever higher, the flames rose. Ever faster, the fire traveled.

Along each vector, the roaming infernos sped. What was once Mason Pawlatowski became the holocaust that barreled west toward the world-famous airport formerly known as Old Orchard. What was once Ethan DeMaris ate its way east toward the North Side of Chicago.

That night, the city would suffer yet again like it had back in 1871, but with bigger explosions, more deaths and even more destruction. Chicago was about to be treated once more to a flaming shit sandwich with extra hot sauce all because of general stupidity and negligence.

***

0305:56 CST –
"Jesus, I think we just cleared the threshold!" the first officer cheered. "We beat it, Rob! We got this by the tail!"

– The Wreck of *United 242* –

The captain of *United Airlines Flight 242* was only half-listening to the good news as he eyed the altimeter with single-minded diligence. Despite the instrument assuring him of the steady lift, he could not deign to trust their luck. After all, the runway behind them looked much like the River Styx.

"Okay, Rob, I'm gonna get on the mic and tell the cabin. They'll love it."

To that, the jet's pilot shook his head. "Just hold on, Matt. Something's wrong."

"What is it?"

"Shit," he hissed under his breath. "I've gotta check with O'Hare. Looks like we're losing fuel."

Shrugging his shoulders, the first officer huffed. "Sure, I guess. Speed's a little fast, but considering the circumstances…"

He ignored his co-pilot, made an arresting gesture with his hand and radioed the traffic control. "Departure, *242* indicates a steady drop in fuel pressure. You guys need to file a report on this. Set us up for an emergency."

United 242 continued to ascend above the engulfed burbs not far below. Even though their lead had instrumental suspicions, those suspicions were correct as flames from the melting tarmac had caught the commercial jet's fuel line during her great escape into the sky. Once again, the element of gas would lead to unmitigated death.

"I've got nothing out of Departure, Matt," the old PNF said. "Can't get them on the horn."

"Try Local," their second officer interjected. "They might be able to take over comm. Tell them what the hell's going on. I confirm the loss too."

Annoyed, the pilot sloughed off that suggestion along with his phones. "No, Ryan. Local's in the middle of Shitter's Ditch by now. If Departure's knocked out, those guys are ashes. And screw Company. Those pukes are worthless."

Their argument was interrupted by the blare of alarms pulsing throughout the fight deck. Angry, red lights met the beat of the klaxons. They could feel it; something horrible was certain to happen.

"Fire report!" the second yelled. "We're on fire! That fat, fucking moron on the ground didn't close the cap. We bought it in the line!"

"No surprise there," his commander said. "Kid was probably barbecued while on the pumps. Poor momma's boy."

"Surely we can shut off the main valves and contain this," the second officer offered. "It'll be tough on the range but we can at least make it to Detroit and do an emergency there."

"Sorry, Ryan," his bellwether moaned, dejected. "The fire's too far dug in. The harder we punch it, the worse it'll get. And stop calling me Shirley…"

That old, flyboy in-joke wasn't so funny now, but Captain Robert Grundle wanted to crack it for what he knew would be one final time. Seeing the altimeter report the loss of air, his heart sunk as he knew this would be his last flight ever.

Alongside the ring of the alarm, yet another warning beeped from the instruments, singing songs of the engines' critical failures. One by one, the turbines combusted as the fiery outbreak molested them.

"We've lost the engines!" the flight engineer cried. "That explains why we're getting no lift."

"I know this, Ryan," the doomed aviator spat. "Knock it off."

"Maybe we can switch to auxiliary and land this in a field. Indiana?" the second-in-command suggested. His voice reeked of false hope.

Grundle growled. "That isn't responding either."

With a rapid, yet steady descent, *United 242* slid through the smoke-choked skyline en route to a grand structure once known as the world's tallest building. The craft's kiss to its monumental architecture was unavoidable.

"We can't clear Willis!" his copilot howled.

"Jesus Christ Superpimp…"

IMPACT.

At 0315:32 CST, the flight of *United 242*, out of O'Hare did make collision with the sixty-third floor of the Willis Tower in Chicago, Illinois. Not one of her two hundred thirty passengers and crew survived.

***

"Pow, bitch! Crossbow!"

-Vampire Slave Building is Crumbling-

Dookie "Baby Duke" Madison wasn't lying. He had acquired such an antique weapon for the fight. Due to his condition of primordial dwarfism, Mr. Madison only weighed in at nineteen pounds, seven ounces and stood a solid twenty-seven inches at the tender age of twenty-two. A tiny thug, but a thug, nonetheless, Dookie had to resort to the handheld version of the archaic killing machine for the battle at hand. The recoil of the guns that his brothers-in-arms would use under normal circumstances proved much too fierce for his unnaturally small frame.

As the gangland kerfuffle between the Conservative Vice Lords and the Latin Kings raged across Lower Wacker Drive, just within the late-night shadow of the titanic Willis Tower, the diminutive crime boss let loose a bolt from his lowrider's sunroof. The missile sailed true and burrowed through the right eye socket and into the brain of one Hector Asuncion de la Cortez, L.K. Lieutenant.

"I fuckin' *love* this thing!" the pipsqueak pimp marveled as his quarry wailed in mortal pain. "How you like me now, chump? Two feet tall, one foot of dick! Load me up for another, brother!"

"You got it, boss," his subordinate down in the passenger seat murmured.

As the young Vice Lord worked the retention spring of the crossbow, a horrid, violent roar screamed through the sky of Chicago's late watches. The pavement grumbled in resistance to the atmosphere's breach. Even the return bursts of the Latin Kings' volley of automatic weaponry took pause.

"What the fuck, Nut Bone!" Dookie barked. "Stop bumping the hydraulics, you punk!"

"Ain't doing nothing, boss," he responded. "Man, I think *Chicago* is shaking!"

"What the…"

High above the streets of the world's murder capital, a phoenix forged of heavy metal and fiberglass tore through the night air and into the heart of the towering monstrosity built in the honor of commerce and capitalism. The explosion was so grand, so immense, that the shockwave absorbed its very sound. Glass and mortar rained down hellfire onto the city it had loomed over for so many decades.

"Did you see that?" the little Vice Lord general squealed. "Some asshole just nine-elevened the shit out of the Sears Tower!"

"Uh, don't you mean the *Willis* Tower?" his driver corrected.

Enraged, Baby Duke plopped back into the car's plush rear seats. "What-the-fuck ever, you pedantic prick. We gotta get our asses out of here! Put your foot in the tank, soldier! Put your foot in the *tank*!"

With peeling white walls, the lowrider passed a bewildered German couple dining at an all-night hotdog stand. How unlucky of them to be touring Chicago on that fateful, late night.

"*Gott im Himmel*!" the young, Teutonic imports screamed. "*Einstuertzende Neubauten*!"

Before the fashionable pair could break away for safer pastures, a chunk of floor sixty-three, about the size of a Ford F-150, crushed their pleas for help. The hapless hotdog vendor was flattened as well along with a teacup Pomeranian named *Schtroomf* that the German woman had nestled within the bowels of her expensive Gucci purse.

The blaze raged on and on. As the city of Chicago, in all her wisdom, had decided to lay-off all but two members of their fire department, no first-response assistance would be en route. No neighborhood would be allowed to stand unscathed that night. From O'Hare in the west to Navy Pier in the east, a festival of flame and carnage was celebrated under the shimmer of uncaring starshine.

As for Baby Duke, he awoke later that morning to the thick smoke which filled his Woodlawn Avenue tenement, not far off the Green Line. Sure, the Latin Kings had failed to defeat him, but Mother Nature proved to be one bad-ass bitch.

***

"President Cyrus!" Jensen alerted. "We still need to know about the situation with Chicago. The politicos are expecting a press conference with you. It could be terrorists!"

-United States Wrecking Ball-

Air Force One purred through the early morning hours without worry, far away from the Great Chicago Fire of 2023. Its commander-in-chief was not only the second female President of the United States, but the youngest, as the position's age of candidacy had been reduced to twenty-five during her electoral run.

"Uh, *yeah*," she snarked at her secret service director. "I'm, like, totally writing a new pop song, okay?"

Jensen grabbed on to the large, scale-model, blue-silver wrecking ball which hung smack-dab in the middle of the jet's conference room. "But Madame President! The Willis Tower has been reported destroyed and most of the city is engulfed in flames! We need to act now."

Cyrus clucked. "And I need to record a new album. Besides, I totally hate Bruce Willis, anyway. *Die Hard Part Twelve* sucked a massive penis. Here, you *have* to hear to my new hit single, *Krokodil*! Just listen to the chorus… now with autotune!"

With the snap of her immaculate manicure, the conference room morphed into a disco. A stroboscopic laser-lightshow filled the cabin and the sound system thumped through the fuselage at one hundred thirty-five beats per minute.

"K-R-O-K-D-I-L!

Come on, get your krokodil!

Cheap as dirt.

Take it light.

Smack it up

And feel the bite!

"I got my crew,

I'm looking fresh.

Krokodil will melt your FLESH!"

She tossed her mic over her shoulder and cared not that it landed in the presidential wetbar. "Pretty freakin' dope, huh?"

Jensen paused. "Er, yes, Madame President. It had a killer hook with slammin' beats."

She crossed her arms with pride. "Yeah, that's what I thought, bitches. I had five songwriters composing it. Including *Carly Simon*!"

"Madame President?" Jensen raised his hand in hopes to grab her deficient attention. "Isn't Carly Simon dead?"

"No, you're thinking about Elton John. And good riddance, too. He was a total asshole. But not as bad as that dumb trollop, Porky Gag-Me I took on for VP. Damn, that girl got *fat*!"

The primadonna president grabbed her tight abdomen and thrust out her ophidian tongue. "Ew, I'm totally starving. Let's fly over to Cali and get an In-Out/In-Out burger. I can always puke it up later. Hell, yeah! Tax dollars hard at twerk. Get it?"

Forlorn, the director lowered his head. "Yes, President Cyrus. I'll inform the captain…"

"Whoo-hoo! Hail Satan!" she cheered.

The airborne headquarters of the United States' dearest leader and former childhood popstar banked westward toward California on a mission for sustenance. As for Chicago, such a matter was not its priority. That once-great city continued to burn as *Air Force One* sped over the Rocky Mountains into the blue gloaming of a brand new day.

An Elementary Contract

Becky Flade

Galen glared at her watch and frowned. She was going to be late. She hated being late. It was unprofessional. The rain that had beat down on her for the last thirty minutes was relentless. Her clothes were soaked through to the skin and her hair was plastered to her skull in what she was sure was an unflattering fashion. Her ice-pick heels were in the car –- she preferred to drive in the comfort of her fuzzy Uggs and she suspected the expensive boots were ruined as the entire shoulder of the road was one large puddle and she sloshed whenever she shifted her weight. Tonight was not going as planned, she thought.

Twin beams from an approaching vehicle lit up the dark road and elongated her shadow. As it neared, it slowed. She shielded her eyes and stepped further into the shoulder of the road as the car pulled in behind her. It was a 2013 Aston Martin. Galen bit back a smile. The driver's side door opened. A thin man with a pinched face and flat eyes wearing an expensive suit under a long rain coat stepped out.

"What seems to be your problem, honey?"

"Thank you for stopping," she gushed. "I thought I caught a flat and pulled over to check it. But like a ninny, I locked myself out of the car and locked my cell phone inside."

She stayed where she was while he peered into the window. She knew her purse lay in full view on the passenger seat, that her keys dangled from the ignition and that her cell phone sat cock-eyed in the cup holder. He even tried the door. It was locked. Then he eyed her. His gaze lingered on the expanse of exposed leg and her bosom. His flat eyes took on a glimmer that was frightening.

"Where are you headed?" he asked. His voice had taken on a husky, almost menacing tone.

"Office party. We're announcing a new merger." she pouted. "It's mandatory and I'm late. I'm going to catch hell from the boss," she whined. Then glanced down at herself. "And I look a mess."

"You look okay to me, sweetheart." He smiled and she made herself return the gesture. "I can give you a ride to where you're going or I can call Triple A for you and you can continue to wait here in the rain."

She chewed on her lip. She looked from his car to hers and glanced at her watch anxiously. "I'd really appreciate the ride, thank you. I just can't lose my job. The party is at the Hilton on Seaside."

"That's right on my way." He smiled as he put his hand on the small of her back and led her the few feet to where he'd parked.

"This is a gorgeous car," she told him.

"Yes, she is."

"I'll ruin your upholstery." She hesitated, pulling back. "I'm all wet," she explained. He took off his coat and wrapped it around her. Then he winked at her and bent low to grasp the door handle. Quickly, and with great force, she jabbed a razor-sharp blade into the exposed soft space where his jaw and neck met, and severed one of his jugular veins completely. He fell with an almost anticlimactic splash to the ground, shielded from the road by his own vehicle.

Galen bent down beside the dying man. She rinsed her hands and her blade in the runoff that was forming the puddle where he lay. He'd stopped jerking. It had taken less than two minutes for him to die. She straightened, palmed the key fob to her vehicle, unlocked it and popped the trunk. She placed his coat and her ruined boots in a bag, slammed the lid and ran barefoot to the driver's seat of her car.

Ah hour later, she strolled out of the ladies' room in a wildly popular dance club. Bodies pressed in on one another, moved in rhythm with the bass pumping throughout the dimly lit room. She felt her blood thicken and her heart pulse in time with the music. She liked it here. She made a mental note to organize a girls' night out sometime soon with friends. It had been too long since she'd drunk until her head swam and she'd danced with abandon.

She grabbed a martini from the bar, but it was only artifice, and continued to weave through the crowd. Her target would be on the second level – in the VIP lounge.

She spotted him easily enough. He was surrounded by people, men and women alike. As far as she could tell, he only had one bodyguard with him. The rest of his entourage looked to be comprised mostly of desperate fools looking for a tiny crumb of affluence to fall their way. She curbed the need to sneer at the lot of them and cautioned herself to stay on task. And task number two for this evening was far more challenging.

Abram Goraya, the only son and heir to the Goraya media empire, was an internationally known playboy. He went through lovers like most men did disposable razors. He liked to party – hard – with alcohol and drugs, but never to excess. His sole vice was thrills: fast cars, gambling, public sex, extreme sports. If it could get him killed or arrested, it was for him. But daddy's money kept him out of prison and so far, out of a coffin.

And he was highly competitive.

Galen lingered near the bottom of the staircase to the VIP lounge, close to the velvet rope that served to separate the masses from the elite partygoers and gyrated delicately to the music. One of a small band of women already dancing there complimented Galen's shoes and after Galen had bought the group a round of drinks, she was welcomed to join them. She danced and kept an eye on the stairs.

When Abram's younger, less wealthy but more attractive, cousin, Zachariah, approached the steps, she intentionally moved so that he bumped into her knocking her drink to the ground and shattering the glass. The young man smiled and blushed as he apologized. Galen laid a hand on his chest and leaned into him. She flirted heavily and was pleased when his blush deepened. He invited her to join him on the second level and the women cheered her on when he took her hand.

She followed him up the stairs. They sat together on a small chaise directly across from Goraya. She couldn't have asked for a better seat.

The volume of the music required they keep their bodies close and their heads together, giving the impression of instant intimacy. She kept touching Zachariah, laughing and looking into his eyes. When they rose to dance, Goraya rose as well and crossed the narrow distance. He rudely pulled his cousin aside. She stood by unable to hear what they were saying, reading their expressions. Zachariah looked angry, then defeated. He kissed the back of her hand and departed without a word.

It had taken far less time than she'd anticipated.

Goraya smiled at her with what she guessed was meant to be a winning expression. She found it calculating and the man assuming. Had she been here for personal reasons she'd have left already. It never occurred to the man that she wouldn't want to be passed off. She smiled back. He grasped her by the elbow and nodded toward the divan where he had been reclined, but she needed to get him away from his guard and complete the contract as quickly as possible. The more time she spent with Goraya, the more she risked being photographed by the paparazzi that dogged him.

She shook her head and pouted. Galen leaned in, pressed her body to his, pillowed her breasts on his chest and in a shout that sounded like a whisper, told him, "I want to dance. I want to feel your body against mine."

Goraya chuckled and ground his pelvis into her. She gritted her teeth while smiling provocatively. He led her to the top of the stairs; then frowned and shook his head when the guard moved to follow. Galen leaned into him again and pressed her palm to the groin that was clearly his pride. When the man tried to insist, Goraya snapped his fingers and pointed to the ground like one would tell an errant dog to stay. The guard did as he was told, but she caught the ticking muscle in his cheek that showed his irritation.

They blended into the throng of dancers and began moving as one. He was an excellent dancer. It was difficult not to become aroused as she thrust herself along the corded muscles of his thigh. As they danced, Galen pulled him further into the crush until they were in the center of the lights. Her pulse thrummed. It was dizzying and she'd only pretended to sip her martini. She suspected Goraya had enjoyed a little cocaine earlier this evening. She laid her hand over his heart. She'd been right. It pounded.

Now. She slowly slid down his body. When the fly of his slacks was at eye level, she looked up at him and licked her lips suggestively. Goraya smiled wickedly, raised both his hands over his head and shouted, "Yes!"

With the same speed and skill she'd displayed on the side of the road that same evening, Galen sliced the femoral artery as she spun up and around Goraya. Then she embraced him from behind. She held him up in what looked an intimate dance and swayed with him as he bled out on a crowded dance floor. When the song ended, he lay dead and she was gone.

***

Galen parked beside her glistening Nissan Coupe and closed the garage door remotely before exiting the sedan she'd bought the day before. There hadn't been a change of title yet and she planned to resell it. The guy she'd bought it from thought it was a gift for her boyfriend – if any women responded to the ad she'd simply say the car was already sold. Simple enough, she'd done it before. She retrieved the bag from the trunk. Then she stripped off the dress, including, and with a contended sigh, the push up bra, padded panties and corset she'd worn to adjust her curves. She stared mournfully at the heels she did like and then stuffed them with the clothes inside the bag before dropping it by the back door. She slipped surgical booties on her bare feet, and carrying only her purse, entered the kitchen.

Without turning on a light, she paused by the dishwasher and slipped her favorite killing blade in with the forks, spoons and other remnants of her evening meal, then continued on. She strode through the split-level in the dark, tossed her purse on the storage chest at the end of her bed and turned into the master bath. Light illuminated the room from discreet architecture. Her image was reflected in the mirrors that filled the walls. Galen inspected herself, turning this way and that, looking for signs that she'd cut or otherwise incriminated herself. She saw nothing and nodded.

First, she removed the contacts that had turned her blue eyes brown. Then with special soap she erased the stage make-up that hid the freckles she hated, had added a beauty mark and dramatized her eyebrows, which had given her a more Eastern and less Irish complexion. Then she removed the extensions that had turned her chestnut bob into nearly waist length tresses. It took her some time, much longer than it had taken her to end two lives, but when she was finished, she smiled genuinely for the first time in hours at the face staring back at her. Then she got in the shower, booties and all.

Later, curled up on the couch in comfortable pajamas with her laptop and an orange Popsicle, she watched the news report on the roadside murder of Senator Collazo two towns over. Without a tickle of remorse or any other emotion she changed channels until she found another report on the murder of playboy Abram Goraya the next county over.

"Authorities were following all leads," was the official party line on both stations; Galen knew that meant they had nothing. After putting up an ad for the sale of the sedan, she checked her account in the Caymans and smiled.

***

Galen stood at the kitchen window, framed by the early morning sun as it shone through delicate curtains. She sipped a steaming mug of coffee and watched unaffected as the garbage men picked up three bags from her curb and tossed them in the back. She stayed there until the evidence from last night was crushed along with the week's used coffee grounds and her neighbor's cat's litter. Satisfied, she put her mug in the dishwasher and turned it on. She put on a fresh pair of booties before she stepped into the garage and locked the kitchen door behind her.

She stood on the threshold and visually inspected the room. She didn't see anything out of place; nor did she see anything that shouldn't be there. She was aware that there was always the chance she'd tracked in fibers or microscopic traces of blood; things she couldn't see with her eyes that a scientist could find. But she also knew what the likelihood of any law enforcement team linking any of her kills to her was. They'd need probable cause to get the warrant. And that wasn't going to happen. *That's because I'm careful*, she thought to herself.

Carrying her shoes, she approached her coupe. She grinned as she glanced her hand over the hood. It was her only indulgence, this car. Her house was nice but well within her public means. She dressed and vacationed within that persona as well. But this car and those that came before it, she splurged on. Driving fast to loud music made her happy and she had the tickets, always paid on time, to prove it. Not punching the accelerator while on a job was a constant struggle in restraint. But Galen won – every time.

She sat sideways in the driver's seat. She removed one bootie, tossed it to the concrete floor and put on her shoe. Then she repeated the process with the other foot. Confident she hadn't tracked anything into her baby, she opened the garage door and reversed out into the street. Once she was on the highway, she hit the gas and the radio.

She parked in her assigned spot and checked her watch. *Right on time, as usual.* It had occurred to her on more than one occasion that if anyone ever wanted to take her out she'd be more than an easy target. With the exception of the contract work she engaged, she was a creature of habit and it wouldn't take much surveillance to learn her schedule. She shrugged. Everyone had a time and a price. She hoped when both hers came it was quick and expensive.

She popped out of the car and strode into the ugly brown building as she had the day before and would the day after. Some smiled and nodded. Some wished her a good morning. But all were completely ignorant as to what she did in her free time. She loved that.

Galen pushed the door open and walked to her chair with innate authority. She set her purse in the same desk drawer she always did. She popped open her briefcase, pulled out her day planner and the papers she would need for the day. She laid them on her blotter and arranged everything carefully. When it was exactly how she wanted it to be, she placed her case on the floor beside her desk to the side against the wall where it wouldn't be a tripping hazard and took her seat. She glanced at the clock, then her watch, nodded, looked up and smiled warmly.

"Good morning, class. I hope you all slept well because today is going to be a big one. We're starting the multiplication tables." She paused. "It's going to be a killer."

Milk and Cookies

M.J. Sydney

Little Johnnie waited for his father to pass out on the sofa. He always slept there, insisting Johnnie use the only bedroom in the house. It was easier to keep him under control and out of sight. His father was on his eighth beer, which meant he would be out in twenty minutes. Maybe less.

The bedroom door creaked open as little Johnnie turned the knob. One eye peaked out through the small crack and confirmed his father was asleep. He pushed aside a small pile of clean shirts and socks from the corner of his closet until he found his favorite cereal bowl – the one with the blue teddy bear that had *BABY* written around the rim in green and yellow letters. It was nestled safely in the corner where he hid it after his mother's funeral last year. "You're not a baby, throw it out," his father demanded. It was the only memory little Johnnie had left of his mother. Everything else his father stuffed in boxes and had taken to the dump the same day they threw her away in the big hole.

"You need a special plate. Mine's purple," Suzie told him at recess. "And some yummy cookies. And a tall glass of cold milk, but not chocolate. Santa doesn't like chocolate milk, only chocolate cookies." With his bowl in one hand, Johnnie unzipped his backpack with the other and pulled out a wadded-up napkin. He unwrapped the two chocolate chip cookies Suzie gave him from her lunchbox and put them in his special bowl. One of the cookies looked like a mouse bit off the edge where the corner of his library book bumped against it. *There, now he won't see it*, little Johnnie thought as he covered the smashed edge with the other cookie.

His left eye peeked through the open doorway one more time to make sure his father was still asleep before he opened the door just enough to squeeze through. Little Johnnie tiptoed to the kitchen and filled the empty chili can from dinner with milk then tiptoed back to his room. He knew his father wouldn't wake up – he never did – but he couldn't take the chance of his father seeing him out of his bedroom or finding his present for Santa.

Suzie said Santa knows everything about all little kids so he'll know to look in my window, little Johnnie thought as he set the bowl of cookies and can of milk on his windowsill. It was the only safe place he could leave it where his father wouldn't know. "Santa ain't real, boy. And if he was, why the hell would he come see you? Get outta here and go to bed," his father said when he asked if he could leave milk and cookies for Santa. Little Johnnie knew the punishment for disobeying his father but he didn't care if he was locked in his room or got the belt. All the other first-graders left milk and cookies and Santa came to visit them.

He fell asleep snuggling with his mom next to the fireplace, watching the Christmas tree lights flicker and waiting for Santa to come fill the stockings with fun and yummy treats, just like Suzie said she snuggles with her mom on Christmas Eve.

***

Little Johnnie left milk and cookies in his window every year for the next four years. Santa never came. Determined to get it right his sixth-grade year, Johnnie filled his teddy bear bowl with unwanted sugar cookies he confiscated from his classmates in the school cafeteria. At the risk of a weeklong lockdown in his bedroom, Johnnie borrowed his father's tall beer mug, filling it to the brim with cold milk.

He looked up from the kitchen to see his father still sprawled on the sofa, an empty beer can in hand, and nearly a dozen more scattered on the floor next to him. Johnnie set the paper origami tree he made in art class on the card table next to the kitchen. It was the closest thing they had to a dinner table although his father was the only one allowed to eat there. He arranged the bowl and mug as far under the paper tree as they would fit and went to bed dreaming.

Santa crawled in through his bedroom window. It was a tight fit, but he squeezed through. Santa looked around the room and was about to leave when he noticed the bedroom door was cracked open. He found the milk and cookies under the paper tree. Santa smiled and rubbed his belly as he took the last bite of sugar cookie. He brushed the crumbs from his beard and reached into his red velvet bag, pulling out a shiny blue and green package with gold letters spelling out JOHNNIE. A white-gloved hand reached under the tree, now tripled in size and adorned with a string of flickering lights. Johnnie heard the toilet flush, followed by the sound of crashing furniture and shattering glass. Santa looked angry and started to yell.

"Get out here, boy!"

"Yes, father." Johnnie hurried out of bed and stood in his bedroom doorway looking at the floor, as he'd been instructed to do when his father called for him.

"Milk and cookies? You fool. Ain't you too old for fairy tales?" his father yelled.

"Yes, father."

"Clean up your mess and do it quickly."

"Yes, father."

Johnnie picked up shards of glass from the milk-filled beer mug, soaked up the milk and soggy cookies with an old shirt and retrieved the card table from the other side of the living room, setting it upright in its proper place near the kitchen. *Maybe father is right. There is no Santa Claus. And if there was, why would he come here anyway? Father probably told him how bad I am*, he thought while cleaning up the shredded origami tree and what was left of his smashed teddy bear bowl. None of the other sixth graders still believed in Santa, they all said Santa

63

was for babies. Except Cindy Lou, but she wasn't like the other twelve-year-olds. As he secretly shoved the last few remnants of his bowl in his pocket, Johnnie heard the eleven o'clock news reporter reveal the headlines for the nightly news.

"Hey boy, there's your Santy Claus. All over the TV! Looks like he ain't comin' for you again this year," his father laughed and opened another beer. Johnnie didn't dare look up or respond, but listened to the reporter as he pretended to wipe up more milk.

"…identifying himself only as Santa Claus has been arrested in the slaying of a Midland family earlier today. Police report six family members were found amputated in their beds. Investigators found the missing limbs in the kitchen, which appeared to have been repainted with the victims' blood. Neighbor's reported seeing a suspicious man dressed in a red Santa suit flee the house and run down Portland Avenue where police apprehended…"

"You clean up your mess yet, boy?"

"Yes, father."

Disappointed that Santa wouldn't come again this year, Johnnie went to bed dreaming of blood and bones. *Santa doesn't like milk and cookies*, he thought.

***

The idea first came to him over summer break. Spending all summer in his room while his father sat on the sofa and drank gave Johnnie plenty of time to think and plan. He wrote letters to Santa, which he would ask Cindy Lou to mail for him once school started. Cindy Lou dropped her books in the hallway once last year and everyone laughed, kicking her books and papers down the hallway. Johnnie had felt bad seeing her plop down on the floor in the middle of the hallway crying and offered to help her.

As he chased the scattered papers down the hall, a letter she was writing caught his attention – it started, "DEAR SANTA CLAUS." When he asked her about it, Cindy Lou said she's been writing letters to Santa every year since she was four and every year she woke up to find everything she asked for under the tree.

Johnnie's letters didn't ask for toys or video games. He only wanted Santa to come to his house. "He'd been a good boy," he said, he knew he had. His father hadn't taken off his belt or locked him in his room for at least six months now. He apologized to Santa for getting it wrong for so many years and promised he would get it right this year.

When school started in the fall, he gave Cindy Lou the letter addressed to Santa at the prison and asked her to borrow a postage stamp. Cindy Lou was happy to return the favor and didn't question why it was addressed to the prison and not the North Pole. Johnnie told his father he had to stay after school every day to work on a school project. Two hours every day he spent at the public library, researching and learning everything he could about anatomy, raising livestock and stain removal. What he couldn't find from books, he found online, including a simple stocking pattern he printed out and hid in his math book.

Johnnie spent hours in his bedroom fitting the pieces of his teddy bear bowl back together with some glue he brought home from art class. He glued together the stocking pieces he cut from a flannel button-up shirt and faux fur hood he brought home from the lost-and-found at school. The knife he swiped on the sharpening stone ten times each night before bed came from the dollar store, which he bought on his way home from the library with the money he got from Cindy Lou. He told her he needed to borrow a couple dollars for lunch since his father just lost his job. She believed him. He kept the knife on the top shelf of his closet next to the drying stocking and bowl. By Christmas Eve, he was ready, positive Santa would visit him this year.

As he listened under the door, Johnnie heard the news anchor's opening announcements for the eleven o'clock news intermingled with his father's snoring. He sat at the door and waited, listening, knowing he had only one chance to get it right.

"One year ago today, a man known only as Santa Claus was arrested after neighbors identified a big man in a red suit fleeing the home where a family of six was brutally murdered. After prosecutors had failed to provide adequate evidence to charge the man with murder and after undergoing an extensive psychological evaluation, a judge ordered the immediate release of Santa Claus early this afternoon pending further evidence of his involvement in…"

Johnnie retrieved the knife and bowl from the top shelf of his closet and silently made his way to the kitchen to retrieve the beer can he hid under the sink, the top cut perfectly straight and level. It only took him seven cans to get the slicing motion perfect. He set his bowl and makeshift cup on the beer can-lined coffee table and watched his father lie on the sofa snoring. There wasn't much time left. He had to be ready for Santa.

One swift slice across the right side of his neck was all it took. Johnnie jumped back in surprise. He froze, holding the knife at his side, expecting his father to stumble off the sofa and reach for his belt. He didn't. He thought he heard his father yelling. *What are you doin' boy! Get outta here and go to bed!* He didn't. The snoring stopped and his father lie there motionless, much the same as when he passed out in drunkenness, only silent. The sudden realization of what he had done hit him like a bolt of lightning. Johnnie grabbed the beer can cup from the coffee table, holding it against his father's bleeding neck. He watched as blood filled the can, pouring from the jugular and down his father's shoulder.

Johnnie set the can on the floor; his eyes locked on his father's, and reached down to pick up a limp hand dangling over the edge of the sofa. He held up each finger in turn, carefully pierced the skin and cut around the joints, first exposing the bone. Using the beer can-covered coffee table as a cutting board, Johnnie pushed the knife through the cartilage, separating each finger like a chicken wing. Disjointing the toes in the same manner was easier and faster after having ten fingers worth of practice. The hardest part was getting the toes up on the coffee table cutting board.

With the last pinky toe removed, Johnnie laid the knife down on the coffee table, knocking over the last beer can, and washed himself up in the kitchen sink. He rinsed off the freshly cut cookies and stood them up neatly in his teddy bear bowl – fingers on one side and toes on the other. The finger- and toe-nails lining the top of the bowl made a wavy pattern. *A nice touch*, Johnnie thought.

He smiled as he opened the freezer door and took out the last blue-raspberry popsicle – the one his mom promised to give him if he was good for daddy until she got back from the store. Only she never came back and his father wouldn't allow him in the kitchen.

He took the old, frozen popsicle and the fresh, warm milk and cookies back to his bedroom. Johnnie left the milk and cookies on the windowsill, just as he had every year. Except last year. That was a mistake. Johnnie hung his stocking from a hook centered between the teddy bear bowl and beer can. *I've been good*, he thought, licking the sticky blue-raspberry treat and admiring his gift for Santa. He gazed out the window, up at the stars, and made a wish before crawling into bed.

As he drifted off to sleep, the night stars twinkled and glistened in the darkness behind closed eyelids. He heard the clickity-clacking of reindeer hooves across the roof and Santa's sleigh landing with a swoosh. Santa held Johnnie's letter in his hand as he came in through the bedroom window. Santa filled the stocking with candy and…

A rush of cold air swept across Johnnie's face, followed by the sound of his bedroom door hitting the wall as it slammed open, jolting him upright in bed.

"Don't you know stockings get hung by the fire, boy?" said a raging voice from the doorway.

"Yes, father." Johnnie sat up rubbing his eyes into focus.

A tall, burly silhouette of a man in a red suit stood in the doorway laughing and holding up the blood-dripping knife Johnnie left on the coffee table.

"You came," Johnnie said with a smile.

Cold Compensation

Dionne Lister

Tuesday

Dr. Fredricks leaned over the bed in the recovery ward. His thumb held open the patient's eyelid as he shone a light in one blue eye, then the other. He stood and rubbed at his lower back. "Nurse, when the patient is lucid, call me and give her a popsicle. I have to prep for the next surgery."

"Yes, Doctor."

When Dr. Fredricks turned to leave, he spied Jerry, the young orderly, emptying the non-surgical waste bin, his lank, dark fringe falling to cover his eyes. *Unkempt imbecile*, he thought. The doctor, whose own graying hair was oiled and combed back to hug his scalp, scowled at Jerry before pushing through the swinging doors.

Jerry stopped what he was doing and looked up to see Dr. Fredricks leaving. He watched the bald spot on the back of the doctor's head as he disappeared through the doors. Wanting to go and see how the doctor's latest patient was doing, he gritted his teeth because he knew that the nurse would just shoo him away — others thought of him as the mildly-retarded, obsessive, overweight charity case, only working at the hospital because his grandmother's best friend worked in their recruitment department.

Strangling the throat of the plastic garbage bag before twisting it and tying it in a knot, he dumped it on his trolley and wheeled it out of the ward, his clubfoot causing him to limp. He wasn't stupid like everyone assumed, and before this week was over, he would prove it to all of them.

Karen fought the tiredness and blinked a few times before her eyes agreed to stay open. The operation was over and she'd survived. A wan smile showed her relief.

"So, she's awake. Great to have you back. I'm sure you're thirsty after the anesthetic. Suck on this." The nurse, so thin that the lines and sharp angles of her face and shoulders made her seem severe, held a green popsicle to Karen's mouth. When the ice block was firmly in her mouth, the nurse said, "The doctor will see you a bit later. Can you hold it by yourself? There you go. I'll be back soon."

Karen watched the nurse return to her station. When the nurse got there, she said something to another nurse and they both looked in her direction. Shivering at their stares, she suddenly thought that maybe her operation hadn't gone well. *What weren't they telling her?*

Wednesday

Dr. Fredricks straightened his tie and peered across his mahogany desk at his next patient. Julie Dern: twenty-four, in excellent health, except for a troublesome bout of endometriosis.

Julie smiled at the doctor. "Thank you so much. I can't tell you how relieved I am that you can perform the surgery. My insurer is so cheap that the other two doctors said my share of the payment would be $3,000. There's no way I can afford that. I can't believe you don't charge any excess."

"At Be Well Now clinic, we just want our patients to get better. I already own a mansion, so why do I need to rip people off?" He spread his hands, as if to say he had nothing to hide.

Julie's short giggle was part nerves and part relief. She had Googled the clinic and found there was only one blog that complained about a complication. "Um, I read on someone's blog that they went in for an ovary removal and left with one less kidney. Is that normal?"

Dr. Fredricks shifted in his seat, his hand moving to his neck before he forced it back down to rest on the table. "That was very unfortunate. If it's the case I'm thinking of, the patient had cancer that spread to the kidney, so we were forced to take it out. She was in shock afterwards and kept blaming us, but if it weren't for me, she'd be dead."

Julie nodded, satisfied. "Okay, then, book me in for this Friday."

The doctor grinned, stood and shook Julie's hand. When she left, he followed her out — it was time to go and check on his patient from yesterday, Karen.

Dr. Fredricks smiled when he saw Karen sitting up eating lunch. "Good afternoon, Miss Simmons. How do you feel?"

Karen brushed a crumb from the corner of her mouth. "I'm a bit sorer than I thought, and the nurse said instead of going home this afternoon, I'll have to stay for another week. Am I okay? What did you find?"

"There were complications during surgery — nothing we did, you understand. Your kidneys started to shut down. When we investigated, only one kidney was functioning correctly. There was scar tissue on the other, and we thought it best to remove it."

The patient dropped her fork. "What the hell? Are you telling me I only have one kidney?"

"I'm afraid so. If we didn't take it out, you might have died or been left with no kidneys. You can function perfectly well with only one and that's much preferable than dialysis."

Karen wanted proof that it had been her kidney's fault and not the doctor's, but how? Then she remembered the waiver form she'd signed. Even if they'd killed her through negligence, no one could sue.

When the doctor walked out, Karen started to cry.

Wednesday night

The flickering luminescence from the big-screen television splattered colorless light on Jerry's features. He stared at the operation unfolding in front of him, every now and then jotting something down on his notepad. Jerry had always wanted to become a doctor, like his father, but no one thought he was capable and they certainly wouldn't waste their money putting him through college. Instead, he had been encouraged to work at the local electronics store that was owned by his uncle. He'd lasted a few months until he managed to convince his grandmother that he'd make a good orderly. His dream had been to help people, and soon, he'd get to do just that.

Jerry opened his eyes wide to make sure he didn't miss what Dr. Fredricks did when he sliced the patient's kidney from its anchor. Yes, that electronics experience had paid off. The cameras he'd secretly installed in the operating room at the clinic were working fine. His confidence grew with each operation he witnessed. He couldn't wait — his first operation was only a day away.

Thursday morning

While Jerry emptied the bin in Dr. Fredricks office, the door opened. The doctor walked in, briefcase in one hand, mobile phone in the other. "Look, Joseph. I know I said I could get two for tomorrow, but I've got one. Any more than that and it's going to look suspicious." He looked up and saw Jerry. "I can't talk now. What? Yes, O positive. Just be ready tomorrow around 11 am. Bye."

Jerry walked up to Dr. Fredricks, who pushed past him to the other side of his desk. He slapped the briefcase on the desktop and noticing Jerry was still there, looked at him. "What do you want?"

"Dad, I know what you're doing. It's wrong. Where's your empathy . . . your ethics?" Jerry briefly met his father's eyes before blushing and looking down.

"You're an imbecile and a coward. If you think I'm doing something wrong, why don't you go tell someone, idiot. As if anyone would believe you. You're living in a fantasy world, Jerry. I'm glad your mother isn't alive to see what a failure you turned out to be. Now get out."

Jerry kept his head down but moved his eyes up to shoot an angry glare at the man who had fathered him. He didn't want to lose his nerve now, not when there was another patient tomorrow — he had looked at her file: Julie. Too late to save Karen the indignity of losing one of her organs, he wasn't going to fail Julie.

The young man limped out of the office, closed the door and checked his watch: 5.15 p.m. He went to his locker and grabbed what he needed. Only forty-five minutes to go. So many things had to go right for this to work, and if it went wrong, well, he would end up in jail — hell, if it went right he would end up in jail. Jerry shrugged and thought *If I don't do this, I'm no better than he is.* His hands shook slightly as he rechecked the items in his bag.

Thursday night

Most of the staff at the clinic had left by 6 p.m., and the few who remained gave Jerry curious glances as he half-dragged his father to the car. One of the security guards asked, "Is he okay?"

Jerry said in between heavy breaths, "Yes. He's just had a few too many." Then he whispered, "It's the anniversary of my mother's death."

"Oh. Sorry 'bout that. Do you need help getting him to the car?"

"Thank you. That would be great."

Late Thursday night

Dr. Fredricks lay still, listening. *Where am I?* he thought, while trying to force himself to wake up. The smell of disinfectant and hay claimed his attention, and he opened his eyes. Dark timber beams and roof trusses loomed above him. This place seemed familiar, but he didn't recognize the white-paneled walls.

At the foot of the bed stood Jerry, looking at a patient chart. Noticing movement, he glanced at his father before writing something in the chart. "I'm so glad you're awake. I wasn't sure if the operation would work, but I had the video playing, just in case I forgot what to do. I'm pretty sure it went well." He nodded to the television behind him before he walked around to one side of the bed and stared into his father's eyes.

"What did you do to me? Is this a nightmare? Are we in the stables?" Dr. Fredricks croaked.

"No, it's all real, and yes, I renovated the tack room. It's important to operate in a sterile environment."

Jerry's father stared back in terror, his mouth contorting in a silent, manic dance.

"I thought you should see how it feels to have something taken from you without your consent. I videoed the operation so you can look at it later and make sure I did everything okay." Dr. Fredricks made a strangled sound. Jerry patted his leg through the covers and said, "Just a minute."

He returned with a green popsicle. "This is your favorite flavor, from what I can remember. Here." He shoved it into his father's mouth, as he had seen his father or the nurses do to the "special" patients in recovery. It's not that Jerry didn't appreciate that his father paid for everything, but selling organs on the black market was evil, in his opinion. The guilt Jerry had felt for being supported by stolen organs, lifted.

Dr. Fredricks raised the sheet and looked down. All he could see were white bandages. "Is this a joke? What did you do — knock me out with Rohypnol and fake the rest? Help me up, for God's sake." He tried to sit. A shooting pain radiated from his abdomen and he dropped back to the pillow, sticky green drips from the ice block plopping onto the white sheet.

"When they came for your kidney, I explained that it would be the last one. Now eat your popsicle."

The patient's wild eyes stared at Jerry, but he obediently sucked the icy treat as tears streamed down his face.

"Oh, actually, they will come back, just one more time. I forgot to tell you; I promised them half of your liver."

In the Tub

Gabino Iglesias

"Joe, come in here with the spatula before you leave for work!"

Dread seeped through Joe. Amanda's shrill voice reached him at the small table in the kitchen and made him realize he'd been hoping to be out the door before her morning constitutional. The thought of fishing her sausage-like turds out of the tub suddenly killed his craving for coffee.

For the fifth consecutive morning, Joe wondered if there was an easy way to tell Amanda she should go back to the water. He practiced starting lines in his head, but they all inevitably lead to anger and the kind of argument that ended in yelled insults and utter nonsense. Despite that, something had to be done. The past three weeks had been rough, and things were only getting worse.

"Joe, what the fuck are you doing? Get your ass in here with that damn spatula!"

All Joe had wanted out of that fateful Friday night was to score some weed, knock back a few beers, forget about the loading docks, and relax. He'd taken the bus down to Morris Heights and walked to the back of the Roberto Clemente State Park. Tony was waiting for him near the same cluster of trees as always. They talked about the cold and how much the Mets sucked. Then Tony left and Joe decided to go for a stroll. That's when he heard a voice coming from the Harlem River. A woman was calling out to him, but he couldn't spot her. The he did. She was in the water. Topless. Her big, round, white breasts were jutting out of the water like fleshy cannons and the mop of bright, red hair on top of her head shone like nothing Joe had ever seen.

The hours that followed were hazy, as if he could only see them through a dirty glass. He'd borrowed a friend's van and, with the help of an old comforter, managed to sneak Amanda into his second floor apartment without being seen. That night was magical. A dream. Love at first sight. They talked for hours as she soaked in his tub. She told him about the most beautiful beaches in the world, unfound treasures in the bellies of sunken ships, unknown fish species from the deep that generated their own light, and about her lifelong dream of living in New York. Joe got drunk on her words and wanted to lose himself in her piercing, emerald eyes. They kissed while the first rays of the morning sun slowly crept in through the kitchen window and bathed the bathroom's white walls with their timid light.

Learning to tell the difference between Amanda's genital orifice and her anus was relatively easy. Figuring out a way to have sex in a minuscule bathroom with a legless woman whose flapping tail knocked down everything that wasn't screwed in place in said bathroom was not. Joe skipped work the next day and ended up sleeping on the cold floor next to the tub. Sadly, what looked like a dream come true soon turned into a nightmare.

Amanda woke Joe up with a shove and asked him for food. She had taken out her green contacts and Joe saw her eyes were a dull brown, the whites full of veins that made him think of bloody eggs. The shiny, red hair turned out to be not so red and her black roots were showing. She looked older than the night before. Worse than that, she looked damaged beyond repair. All men are idiots, and Joe knew that details had escaped him because he was focused on her big, perky breasts. Sadly, the punishing light of day also made the awful scar around each nipple visible.

"Joe, if you don't get this shit outta here in the next thirty seconds I'm gonna start throwing it out into the hallway! You think a lady should be kept marinating in her own shit, you little punk?"

Joe got up, walked to the sink, and dug the spatula from under a pile of dirty dishes. For a second, he thought about grabbing a knife instead of the spatula. His previous girlfriend, a woman with the body of a pancake and a personality to match, had pissed him off plenty of times, but she'd never made him feel like this. He felt broken, abused, drained. His heart was full of rot. The thing in his bathroom was not beautiful or even remotely interesting anymore. Amanda was a dark cloud, a sack of vitriol, a curse, a freak.

"Joe, how many fucking times do I have to… "

"Shut the hell up!"

In three weeks of unrelenting verbal punishment, Joe had never interrupted Amanda before. He always kept his head down during her outbursts, but he'd had enough. Telling her to shut up had probably stung her worse than a slap on the face. The silence coming from the bathroom was far more eloquent than her screaming. It felt ominous. Joe had always thought of his apartment as a cozy womb, and Amanda had violated it with her presence, sullied it with her words, and soured it with her attitude.

The door to the bathroom was open and Joe could smell Amanda before he reached it. The stench of fish and feces made his nose hairs gag. He stood in the doorway with the spatula and looked at Amanda. She was texting someone. Her thumbs tapped the screen urgently and made him think of fat worms having epileptic seizures.

"Who are you texting now?" he asked. He kept his voice neutral. Maybe there was a chance to saving the day and getting out of the apartment soon.

"My friend Rob, the whale. I told you I miss him, but you never listen to me. This is the only way we can stay in touch. Don't tell me you're jealous of a guy I've known all my life."

Joe had thought for a second that asking a question and keeping his voice under control could lead to a civil conversation, but it was obvious his attempt had been futile. He craved a drink, a cigarette, and a bottle of Klonopin.

"Are you gonna get these turds out of here or just stand there like a fucking idiot?"

Joe looked at the tub. Three long strands of feces floated in the water. A fourth was still stuck to her anus, moving in the water like a fat, drunken worm. There were other things in the murky water, but he didn't feel like stepping into the gloomy bathroom and finding out. He threw the spatula at her.

"No, you take them out. If you stretch a bit, you can reach the toilet."

The phone missed his head by a fraction of an inch. It hit the wall behind him and then the floor. He'd spent eighty bucks getting her a waterproof cover. She only used the damned thing to text her old friends and throw it at his head every time they argued. He was tired of it all. Murderous rage took his breath away. He turned, picked up the phone, closed the bathroom door, and went to the kitchen.

Joe sat at the table and smoked three cigarettes down to the filter. Amanda screamed for a while, but went silent when she realized he wasn't coming back. The clock on the microwave read 10:09 a.m. It was too late to go to work. Another day missed. Another chunk of his paycheck lost to Amanda's nonsense. Anyone could load boxes, and someone else was going to get his job if he didn't get his shit together.

Amanda started screaming again. Someone upstairs yelled something back and hit the floor with something heavy. If they called the cops, Joe knew he'd have a lot to explain. He'd been thinking about getting rid of Amanda for a while, but now it was imperative. From his bank account to his living arrangements, there wasn't a single thing in his life she hadn't affected in a negative way. Then Joe heard a buzz.

The screen on Amanda's phone was lit. Joe picked it up and read the message: "Yu knww I have what you need, babay. My dick is alll yours!!!!"

The bad grammar goes to him. The excessive use of exclamation points made him feel insulted. The guy on the other end of this digital flirting was an idiot, and that's exactly how Joe felt. Rob the whale? He had swallowed it. A whale's lack of thumbs didn't even cross his mind. Now he felt cheated and even angrier than before. He'd taken Amanda home and given her a new life, and she had repaid him by cheating on him somehow. He imagined men somehow sneaking into the apartment while he was at work and his blood started boiling.

Joe was rummaging through his kitchen drawers before he realized he was looking for his hammer. He found it and walked to the bathroom. He couldn't give Amanda a second to talk because she'd surely promise something or say something to make him stop, to convince him of giving her another chance. He wasn't in the mood for more chances.

Joe opened the door with the hammer raised. He took three steps into the bathroom and brought it down on Amanda's head. It didn't bounce back like he expected it to do. Instead, it perforated her cranium with a loud crack and stayed there. Amanda's arms moved a little and her tail splashed up and down a few times. Then she was still. Her eyes were open and they looked at Joe, but her mouth wasn't moving, and that was all that mattered. Joe took a deep breath he immediately regretted and sat on the toilet.

The floating jelly sacks floating in the tub had only registered as an anomaly on his peripheral vision, but now they had his full attention. Even in the dark bathroom, the squirming things inside the translucent sacks were visible. Joe looked at Amanda's unmoving tail and realized he was going to have sushi for dinner. Then, with a full stomach, he'd figured out what to do with the eggs.

True Romance

Bradley Sands

A light box and an ironing board fall in love with each other. The man says, "This is not allowed, light box. Your full-spectrum light is supposed to treat my seasonal affective disorder. Don't think you're off the hook either, ironing board. I need you so my clothes won't be wrinkled for when I go to job interviews." The light box and ironing board hug and caress. "I'm going to write a letter to the editor of my local newspaper to express my frustration."

The story gets picked up by the national media, dividing America into two groups: those in favor of object sexuality and those against it. Some argue that object sexuality goes against the laws of reality. Others respond by saying that reality decides upon its own laws—humans don't have the means to determine how reality has chosen to police itself. The Pope enters the conversation through his English interpreter with, "Object sexuality is unchristian." During the presidential election, the citizens vote on a referendum to sanction object sexuality. By midnight, the vote has yet to be decided. Every state except for Florida has finished their count and "no" is only up by twenty-three votes. Someone drops an atom bomb on the Orange State. A group called the American Relationship Association claims responsibility. A civil war breaks out, people die, things blow up, inanimate objects are herded into internment camps. Reality enacts a law requiring itself to party all the time.

The light box and the ironing board snuggle under the covers, lit up in a neon-green afterglow that helps the man find his way to the toilet through a haze of unemployment and seasonal depression.

The Worm Men

Jeremy C. Shipp

The worm men arrive before I finish the apricot-almond clafouti. I bite into the melting flesh of the fruit, and the two men stand in the corner, with their bulky arms crossed over their yellow suspenders. I would offer them leftovers or a cup of coffee, but they won't speak to me. They're trained not to speak to me, I suspect.

"I saw a worm fall from the sky this morning," I say.

One of the men arches an eyebrow, but they don't respond otherwise.

I don't understand why a worm would fall from the sky, but I'm not an expert. Perhaps the clouds themselves have become infected.

After I finish my clafouti, it's my turn to stand in the corner. I don't cross my arms over my chest. I lean with my arm and head against the wall. My mind always swirls a little after dinner. Sometimes my eyes cross on their own accord.

I watch the men as they kneel on the wooden floor, scooping up handful after handful of worms. The slimy insects are nothing like the smiling cartoon worm on front of the men's black shirts. Sometimes the bugs cling together, forming thick strands of writhing flesh.

The sight makes me sick, but I always stand there in the corner of the dining room, leaning, watching. I think about the worm falling from the sky. I imagine a cloud saturated with squirming bugs.

"Thanks for your help," I say.

The men glance at me, and then they sprinkle the purifying dust on the floor. I wish someone would invent a dust that could keep the worms away. But the world is too deeply infested. We summoned the worms with our oil wars and our reality TV shows and our plastic surgeries. There are a thousand reasons for the worms, and there's no going back now.

Thank god for the worm men.

The next day, someone slides a dinner card through the mail slot on my front door. The name MARK STANNING glimmers on the card, handwritten in gold calligraphy.

"Mark Stanning," I say.

The name is unfamiliar, but that comes as no surprise.

For dinner, we feast on oversized mozzarella arepas with summer vegetables and sweet plantains. Mark eats like a cat who hasn't been fed for two days. After he finishes his plate, he looks at me with his bright, green eyes.

"Is there any dessert?" he says.

"First we need to talk," I say. "You need to tell me why you're here."

Mark looks down at his empty plate. "I suppose I'm here because of the field trip. We went to the beach, to explore the tide pools. We saw Cthamalus barnacles and blue-banded hermit crabs and sea hares. We found a large worm washed up on the shore. Bigger than a school bus. Bobby, a boy in my class, he wouldn't stop kicking the worm. I asked him to stop four times." Mark pinches at the edge of his empty plate. "I led the children away from the tide pools, away from the sand. We walked and walked and finally I told Bobby to step forward. I grabbed his arms." Mark holds out his hands, curling his fingers like claws. "I threw Bobby off the edge of a cliff." Mark Stanning glances at me, with a sheepish look on his face. I want him to stop talking, but it's my job to listen. "I managed to throw two other children before the parents got to me and held me down. You should have heard the way the children screamed as they fell into the sea." Mark laughs a little.

"You shouldn't throw children off of cliffs," I say, squeezing my fork. "They must have been terrified, falling so far."

Mark shrugs. "It just happened. Can we have dessert now?"

I try to focus my thoughts on the lemon and raspberry dacquoise waiting for me in the fridge, but I can't seem to move beyond Mark Stanning and his confession. I feel his infected words bouncing around inside my head. I hear the screams of the children as they fall toward the sea, flapping their arms like baby pigeons. I smell the sea air. I feel the worms wriggling between my fingers.

By the time I return to my senses, Mark is already gone. I wonder how long he sat there, waiting for me to snap out of my trance. Maybe he spoke to me. "Martha, what are you doing? Martha, Martha!" But I didn't budge, so he left. He didn't even get any dessert.

I stumble to my fridge, still a little dizzy. I cut myself a slice of lemon and raspberry dacquoise. As I return to the table, I notice the worm man for the first time. Worm men always come in pairs, but today there's only one. He stands in the corner, with his bulky arms crossed over his yellow suspenders. The cartoon worm on his shirt grins at me.

I search the room. Ah, there are worms on the floor again, squirming and clinging together. I turn to the worm man, and I notice that he's not looking through me.

"Would you like some dessert?" I say, holding out my plate.

The worm man uncrosses his arms. "Yeah. Sure."

I always knew that the worm men were physically capable of speaking, but his voice startles me. I turn around quickly and return to the fridge. With a shaky hand, I cut another slice of dacquoise.

The worm man eats in silence, glancing at me every once in a while. He looks worried. Maybe he's not supposed to accept gifts.

"I won't tell anyone about the dessert," I say.

The worm man nods.

After he finishes his meal, he carries his plate to the sink. He returns to the table and carries my plate to the sink as well. He rinses them, staring out the window at my vegetable garden. He places the plates carefully on the marble counter.

"You don't have to do that," I say, after he's finished.

The worm man kneels on the floor and gets to work. He scoops the worms into his black plastic bag. I wonder where the worms will go from here. Maybe they're all taken to the same place, where they cling to one another, forming a mountain of undulating flesh.

I shiver.

The worm man freezes.

"I want to tell you," he says. "But maybe it's not the right thing. But maybe you have the right to know."

He stands and faces me, and I take a step back.

Using his teeth, the worm man takes off his gloves and throws them on the floor. "Why do you think they send people like Mark Stanning here?"

"It's my job to listen to their sins," I say. "I'm here to purify their minds."

"That's not it. That's not what happens." The worm man rubs his forehead. "The people we work for, they know how angry you get. They use that anger. They amplify it when they want you to lose control."

I lean against the wall. "What are you talking about?"

The worm man reaches in his pocket and pulls out a flashlight covered with orange stripes. "You stabbed Mark Stanning with a knife. You stabbed him a lot."

I can feel the worm man's words saturating my mind. I see myself stabbing Mark Stanning again and again. His bright, green eyes plead for me to stop. I hear his screams. I smell his blood. I feel the worms wriggling between my fingers.

I feel myself lost in another cloud, and I don't know how to escape.

As soon as the worm man shines his flashlight in my eyes, I regain my senses. I'm no longer leaning against the wall. I'm holding a knife in my hands, the blade a foot from the worm man's chest. What am I doing? I feel nauseous, dizzy. My eyes cross on their own accord.

"I'm sorry," I say, dropping the weapon.

The knife lands next to Mark Stanning. Mark is lying on the floor, where the worms used to be. What is Mark doing here, covered with blood? Why isn't he blinking?

"What's wrong with him?" I say.

"He's dead," the worm man says, his voice crackling like fire.

"What does that mean?"

The worm man won't look at me. He stares at his black tennis shoes. "I don't really know how to explain it. I deactivated the device in your head. Now you can see the truth. The world is not infested. The worms were never really there."

I touch my face, and I walk outside. I can't look at Mark Stanning and his blood anymore.

Outside, I search for the worm that fell from the sky, and I find a blue bird in its place. She's lying on the grass with her eyes wide open, her wings askew.

I throw her at the sky, but she falls and crashes onto the busy street.

Why won't she fly?

Eyes Wide Shut

Trevor Halliday

A cold wind blowing as the hairs on the back of your neck rise high into the night.

The Bazaar silhouetted against the moonlight.

The clashes of music drifted down from the gathered vendors in the bazaar, dance beats fighting rock n' roll, old theatre hall music drowned by the electronic of the eighties glitz, New Romantic era, and the screams of the people walking through the wares that had been brought together by the bazaar, both faked and released in natural surprise for the unexpected consumer or the streetwise bargain buyer.

Of course, curiosity will kill any cat given half the chance, it will take the snooping nose and cut it clean off, without a second thought about the why and the wherefore, with cold efficiency in a dark night illuminated by the cold staring, emotionless moon.

And so it was that he walked up to the bazaar, the various noises washing over him, trying to delicately pick them apart and be intrigued by the dirty canvas tents, the smell of diesel and candy floss, the white noise of people talking to each other; and entering the arena of the bazaar, taking in the sights that were the foundation of the sounds he laid himself open to the tricks of the trades being plied.

Of course, there were the obvious crowd pleases and pullers, and the moon was clearly unimpressed by these mundane attractions. And yet, making the small perimeter walk around the bazaar, there was something that caught his eye that no one really seemed to be interested in, though as he walked by and tried to penetrate the dark shadows that gathered around the inner layer of the stall, the moon must have decided that this was a moment to pay attention to, for he felt the cold stare of the moon's silvery light upon his back, the hairs on the back of his neck rising in excitement.

He was not surprised by the appearance of an old woman from the depths of the shadows, it was almost pantomime as she reached out and grabbed his arm and stared him in the face, her own graveled features drawing close to his so that he felt her aged breath upon his young, supple skin. It crawled a little despite himself, the proximity between youth and old age causing a static charge that forced him to draw back a little, even as she gripped tightly onto his arm even as he took in her appearance and might have laughed, the red patterned shawl hanging about her head and shoulders like funeral dressage.

'You want your fortune read, lad?' She asked a hint of an order mixed with an attempt at street magic hypnotism in it.

'Er…' He hesitated, the brazen request against his impulse to flee was forced aside by manners instilled in him from his early childhood – he cursed inside even as he gave way to politeness.

But now she had him, and she knew it, and with a soft tug and a silent consent, she pulled him into the tent, both opening the canvas partition and letting it drop back down as he was pulled, no, sucked in, somehow the noise outside became instantly muffled, and his eyes adjusted from the night lights of the bazaar to a soft, red hue given by a lazy, burning oil lamp. In the center of the room there was a small table for two to sit opposite each other and around, and she now pulled him towards it and eased him into the uncomfortable wooden chair.

She circled around him, like a vampire hungry for its prey. Her hand brushed against his shoulder and he felt the cold shiver of "Oh! Why did you not just say no!" resound within his head. With grace defying age the woman moved over to the oil lamp and seemed to smell the oil before she turned the adjustor to dull its soft illumination, and then she returned to the table and sat down opposite him; she smiled mysteriously, knowingly at him, her hands reaching out in offer for him to place his own within hers, and somewhere above him, he wondered if the phantom Sword of Damocles had appeared, ready to come down upon him and kill him right there and then, wielded by the powers of the moon that had led him here, or now, he thought about it, tried to warn him off from such intrepid madness.

"No need to be shy," the woman spoke, breaking the silence; he nodded nervously in reply to her. The old woman seemed then to become distant, even while she sat there holding his hands, as though her soul was drifting away in search of something, and he was forced to wonder if this is what mediums did. His mind raced; surely, if this was what the genuine mediums did as opposed to the fakes who appeared on the telly or gathered in the big circuit halls for money they took from the desperate people wanting some sort of clarification on what lay beyond the mundane and material…

And then he realized what had happened while he had been zoning out; he had left his own body like she had seemed to do to her own. This was quickly followed by the exhilaration of flying as he defied the laws of gravity and made like a superhero soaring through the night sky, the moon casting her silver light down upon him as he imagined the theme music he would have and the girls he could save, and the kisses they would shower upon him.

And the moon smiled, the craters and shadows twisted and turned, transforming themselves into the face he had seated himself before, who in the distance of reality, held his hands as though ready to read his palms. And even though he tried to turn this way and that to fly away from the face, she seemed to grow bigger and bigger now, consuming the field of his vision utterly until he once more felt the touch of her ragged breath upon him.

Her face dissolved from the ancient hag he thought he had seen in reality, into one now of serene beauty, her lips parting to invite him in to this dream world as his flight paused by the moment of (in) decision only he could make now that he was before the moon. Sure, he could go back, never get pulled into a fortune teller's tent again and stay away from the bazaar, and carnivals and fun fairs. Pubs were by far the safer, cleaner vice, if you like, which were easy to understand and know your place within if you were happy to stay ignorant of the truth behind the veils of life.

And yet, here was mystery and intrigue, danger and delusion of a grand scale that defied the senses, all senses, even the common sense that was muffled and buried deep within his psyche now, suppressed by the intoxication of defying the laws of reality.

He drifted forward, his fingers reaching out to touch the giant, sensuous lips before him, her breath a soft wind as her enormous eyes cast down upon him with subtle patience. Only a trace of the visage of the old woman remained around the blurred edges of his vision; a mask she wore no doubt to test and move among the lambs of the world.

Enough.

It was a simple thought. A first thought for the beginning of what was to come, a decision to move beyond the known into the unknown, a brave thought that shed the fears of a mundane existence. A deep breath before the dive into cold waters that should reveal such pleasure and pain as you fall away.

He dived in, and as the shockwave washed over him, the truth beyond the veil assaulted him like all childish nightmares gathered together at one great ball of horror to fall upon you as you hide beneath blankets and clutch your favorite teddy bear; his limbs seemed to seize upon him and lose power, and try as he might to force his will inside those dead limbs as those to clutch at away back, or to find a foothold to brace himself, he fell, locked within the prison of his soul, incapable of movement as powerful forces in multiple presence wrapped about him like a riot of intimidation. His immobility caused panic and his willpower retreated, as psychic voices shouted profanities he could not comprehend.

A lifetime passed as the pressure gouged and tore at his flesh, his blood seeped out upon the non-existent floor that cradled him as he wept good thoughts that betrayed him to these foes. Stripping away all pride and sense of self, if he could have moved, he would have folded himself into a fetal position, hoping, praying that the torment would soon end. But these forces knew of no reason to halt their assault, this fresh soul to feed from was a prize to be possessed and fought over, savage, mental voices ripped now at each other and turned their attention from the feast.

His sense of self crawled weakly back into its mind, and while he tried to open eyes blinded by fear, another thought tried to move a hand, first the right, and then the left, or even flex a toe – but no matter how hard he tried, the power of his foes prevented him retaking possession of his bodily controls. Trying an alternative tactic, he felt strength in his throat, his voice, and urged for help, or pity, he forced his voice into his mouth in hope he could cry out and break this stalemate. But in the rage of voices about him, all he could do was force a soft growl from his throat that died within the unmoving mouth; not even a tremble in his lips could affect any form of parting of his mouth to open and whisper.

Now a face came close, too close to his own. Sweating, fleshy matter, and inside he shied away from the monster, fear rising once again. No strength came from the flight-or-fight instincts he might have hoped would surface; such was the power of the unknown upon his soul as it stood naked in the truth of what lay beyond the lies of societies' beliefs, world views forced upon the unsuspecting, unknowing people who walked through so many illusions in everyday life.

No, here was stark, naked truth, the truth of man's inferiority in the face of what existed beyond the edge of the enlightened perception and the threat of shadows in the night and the revelation of what the myths promoted, there were monsters - unimaginable creations that the perception of genial minds keep at bay by the great mass of minds forcing them out of the reality he had known, and now cherished in a way he could not have appreciated before. The lies existed to keep society safe, kept the monsters chained in a wider world away from the unbelieving. If God existed, he prayed deeply now, converted back into the arms of that heavenly deceit when confronted with these souls that wandered this vagrant, hollow land.

The face that scrutinized him laughed - a terrible wound-inflicting laugh that dripped with madness and slid into his opening mouth, opening against his will, his body not his own, he struggled internally to try and reclaim his flesh from his fear. *How did he break this?* A thought he clung to as the madness dripped in and slid down his throat and sought out the remaining barriers of his consciousness. In panic, he thrashed about mentally, trying to force the face away, to take back control of his arms, to scream for help. Take the control away from this madness he urged. Help! Help! HELP!

Ice-cold pain washed over him, as burning rage twisted inside, the face seemed to draw back. The powerful tempest of fighting around him seemed to falter and surrender his soul as they drew away, fell back, crumbled as the walls of this place dripped and shattered and fell away. His mind moved at speeds unimaginable as he came crashing, splashing back through the unwalked world, and came charged with electrical power back into the real world, his hands still in the hands of the old woman, the cold sweat upon his brow. His hands suddenly back under his control, he felt his grip tighten frantically upon those of the Fortune Teller. *What was she?* He thought the thoughts of a panicked, insane man as he tightened his hold upon her further still; crazed eyes staring into hers in search of answers without giving them voice.

And while he imagined his strength versus hers would be causing her pain, his youth versus her old, cold, brittle bones, she just stared into his eyes as if seeing the truth of his experiences, knowing. Calmly she spoke to him, and slipped her hands out of his grasp.

"You have seen what we see… Have you the strength to go back and stand among us, or will you retreat into your simple life?"

Panting deeply, as he felt the control return to his body; he looked aghast at this woman, his senses reeled as he assessed and processed what he had seen, what he had experienced, what was going on! What had always been going on, what would always go on. This was the fight unseen, the limit of a world hidden within illusions versus the harsh, stark truth. Man was not the apex predator it thought of itself, it was the prey outside of its assembled hunting grounds. The soul was weak, untrained when pressed against the forces outside the shell of day-to-day life, and the lies that secured the shackles forced upon mankind. Fetters bound upon one from an early age with the tales told, the ministry of ordained messages that set the foundation of learning and illusion. The sermons given to dictate a life dressed with lies.

He thought about her question for a second, then instinct kicked in and he abruptly stood up; his chair broke the silence as it crashed to the floor and he looked down upon the old face that stared back up at him expectantly. And then she turned away, seeing within him the answer he was yet to give voice to, the surrender that started to swell within him. She saw it, he knew she saw it, and while he felt ashamed for his weakness, he found strength in the thought of returning to his world – it lay only outside the canvas of the tent, in the enjoyment of trivial matters and working day life. He felt apologetic, despite himself, because he had seen a truth, and felt the pain, and yet he knew he could not stand to see it again without losing his sense of self.

This was the true horror that lived, and it gave him his shame now, for he turned away, the unspoken questions he knew could get answered if he gave them form - he dare not utter. He retreated and cast a glance back at the old woman who remained seated, not watching him leave. Her chains that had drawn him in now retracted, he felt even breath return inside his body. His hand sought out the opening of the tent, pulled it back so he could take his leave, and between breathes, he walked out once more into the myriad lights and sounds of the bizarre, chaotic gathering of entertainment, yet denied to him. In the white noise of everyday folk he felt his thought processes return and the experience within the tent diminish immediately, its threat lessened, reduced to something he could now mock for its circus tomfoolery.

It was the way of the world to trivialize the unknown into the art of deception and crazed thinking, psychic experiences, hauntings, mediums talking to the dead – all of it was the work of jackals and frauds – and so long as you believed that it would be as armor to the veil that kept such a thing hidden in plain sight from your view.

He had escaped; he could easily rebuild the broken walls of his experience to those lies he was born into. He needed to, and with every step he now took away from the tent, was a brick in the wall of denial. Each returning ounce of strength was the cement in which the bricks would hold firm. He cast a quick look at the moon, that anchor that had brought him to this threatened ruin that he had now evaded; he shrugged and turned away. Clouds concealed the moon, a cold was in the air and while he might have enjoyed the fun of the fair, he knew better and chose to leave.

The hairs on the back of his neck had stood to attention, and they had warned him and he had not listened. Now he listened, now he walked with purpose, now he abandoned the bazaar in favor of the firm authority of the mundane.

Back inside the Fortune Teller's tent, the old woman adjusted her shawl, and stood up, sliding her chair back into its place and went to return the fallen chair also. She looked through the mists, her eyes glazed over as she stood there, searching. Her eyes connected to the spirit; she looked down upon the area through the gaze of silver light, the minute souls of men and women moving this way and that in search of nothing more than the shackles that limited their lives. One day more would open to the truth, one day there would be strength enough for man to see what was, not what is told to them. One day, a time would come that the bazaar would not hold to such title and be revealed as what was true…

Closing the Deal

J.C. Michael

He'd been driving for hours. His eyes were sore from concentrating. His back ached. He'd just joined a single carriageway, and the traffic was jammed solid. The rain was coming down, threatening to turn to snow. It was sickening. He just wanted to be at home with the wife and kids, but he had to make the sale, had to close the deal.

Business was hard to come by. Deep down he knew he'd lost his edge, the razor-like keenness of youth dulled and blunted by middle age. The young pups were getting the leads, flirting with Chantel-May on reception to get the names and numbers of those who'd rung looking for advice, and someone to talk too. She filtered the plum calls to whoever was flavor of the week. It was never him. Not that he wanted it to be. He was old enough to be her father, and for all the stereotypes he did fit as a salesman, the smarmy ladies' man had never been one that applied.

He, Ben Wellesley, had been top dog for the past three years. He'd led the sales forces at all his previous jobs, and hit more targets than an Olympic marksman. But it was slipping away. He'd almost missed last month's quota, and was coasting along in fifth place on the sales volume leaderboard for the year to date. It was a malaise he couldn't shake off. He was perpetually tired. The hours away from home. The nights in Travelodge's. The endless motorways. He'd gone from grabbing the bull by the horns, to picking the low hanging fruit. No longer thinking outside the box, simply milking the same clients over and over. And now, with the cutbacks, and downsizing, the specter of redundancy loomed over him like a Dickensian ghost. He'd crunched the numbers in Excel; all the staff were on commission, but his basic salary was higher due to past performance. His length of service wasn't that long, which suppressed the amount which would come his way as part of any severance package. It was a matter of maths and logic; if he didn't keep up he'd be out on his ear. He had to hit the big score, smash the rest of 'em out of the fucking park.

He'd struck lucky. A competitor had let a guy go, a sound bloke he'd worked with a few years back by the unfortunate name of Richard Head. Over a few beers, he'd told Ben about a deal he'd put together just before getting the push. A good package, but one that could be improved. As each pint of bitter brought an increasing tone of bitterness to Dick's condemnation of his past employers, the details of the deal were spilled as readily as the booze spilt down his chin. The company thought it was in the bag and had a good margin on the deal. The Company deserved to be screwed over by some cunt undercutting them. Getting the final pieces of the jigsaw, the right name, number, and email, cost Ben a double Glenfiddich, but it was worth it. A meeting was diarized the next morning to take place within the week. And here he was now, on his way to that very meeting at a pace that would have bored a snail to tears.

The traffic jam edged painfully onwards, the clock ticked incessantly forwards. He'd set out the night before to split the drive. Being away from home was hard, but he never missed an appointment, and wasn't going to start now. Bad weather was forecast so the plan had been for an evening drive on quiet roads, a night in a Premier Inn, and a shorter journey tomorrow. It was a plan which wasn't working out, but rather the delay now, than in the morning. He was a firm believer in "better an hour too early, than a minute too late."

Eventually the cause of the holdup became clear. A Fiat pulling out of a junction hadn't got out in time, and a lorry had ploughed straight into the side of it. The police, ambulance, and fire brigade were all in attendance. A bad sign. Ben's assumption was that somebody must've needed cutting out, and the fact the ambulance wasn't rushing anywhere was more likely than not a negative omen. It was sod's law that Ben's turn off was only a hundred yards further on, and he'd been in the jam for an hour and a half by the time he reached it.

He turned off, but no sooner had he begun to pick up speed when he saw a bloke in a long, black raincoat at the side of the road, a briefcase in one hand, the thumb out on his other. Ever since he'd started working jobs requiring him to clock up a lot of miles he'd made it a rule not to pick up hitchers. He'd seen the Rutger Hauer movie, and the Sean Bean remake, and however confident he was in looking out for himself, it wouldn't do him any good if some psycho pulled a blade, or worse, on him. In Ben's eyes, any guys he saw by the side of the road could look after themselves and walk. The girls should simply know better, and who knew what he could get accused of if he picked up a female roadside wanderer.

Giving lifts was something he'd never done, but tonight he was tired, nodding at the wheel like his head was on a spring. The hitcher looked like he'd just stepped out of his office to hail a cab, not a random ride, and without consciously realizing he was doing it, Ben pulled over and lowered his passenger window.

"Need a lift?" he asked pointlessly as the man peered in at him.

"It would certainly be appreciated. My car broke down back there," a slight twitch of the head back down the way Ben had come, "and I've an appointment to keep. I never miss an appointment."

It was a sentiment Ben could empathize with, and he could hardly drive off now. Leaning over, he opened the door. The stranger eased himself in.

It was a twisty, turny, little country road, not quite wide enough for two cars to pass without causing both drivers to tense up in the expectation that they may forfeit a wing mirror. A Sat-Nav shortcut that would probably take twice as long as the long way 'round. Concentrating on the road helped keep the Sandman at arm's length, but Ben's eyelids remained droopy. After surprising himself by picking up the hitcher, his rational mind had vindicated the decision, deciding that a bit of company may keep him from the land of nod. His passenger offered no introduction, nor thanks, once in the car, so Ben resolved to take the initiative. His profession called for him to be a communicator, so he put his mind in gear, and his mouth into action.

"Well, your driver today is Mr. Ben Wellesley, regional sales director for D.I.S Inc."

He reached over his left arm with his right, and after a momentary pause, the reciprocal gesture was made. Over the years, Ben had learnt to tell a lot from a handshake, and must have shared in hundreds, but the shake felt like nothing he'd ever experienced before. He felt no pressure upon his hand, yet he felt the pace of the one, brisk, shake, the pace controlled by the other man. He felt no warmth, clamminess, cold, nor roughness. He felt nothing. He felt sick. He pulled his hand away and returned it to the reality of the faintly juddering steering wheel. The fleeting sickness was gone.

He was about to say, "And you?" when the man spoke. His voice was soft, and somehow distant.

"I'm a doctor, on my way to see an elderly couple, both over eighty, who live in a farmhouse a few miles ahead. I'll point out the road when we come to it. It's been many years since my last visit, their son died when he was six."

Something about the way the Doctor spoke sent a chill down Ben's spine which he tried to put down to a blend of fatigue, and the weather, but his gut told him something was wrong. He'd always been quick with figures, constantly calculating, and his synapses fired into action calculating that, if a couple in their eighties had lost a child of six, you were surely looking at an event a good quarter of a century ago. Yet his passenger looked not a day over forty. He'd heard of junior doctors, but the figures didn't compute. Either the Doctor was mistaken, lying, or had a damn good plastic surgeon.

The seeds of doubt were now sprouting through the fertile soil of Ben's thoughts like the first shoots of daffodils in spring. He began to wonder if the once-more silent Doctor was a Doctor at all, or a full-of-shit lunatic with Lord knew what in his briefcase. He turned on the blower in an effort to wake himself up, his thoughts racing but as if through tar. Everything seemed a struggle, his mind torn by an energized lethargy. He didn't ask if it was okay to turn the blowers to full. Why should he? It was his car. But he did ask if the alleged Doctor minded having the radio on. The Doctor ran his hand through his short, black hair, squeezing the rain from it. The water ran down his face like tears as he uttered a single word: No.

The sound of the news filled the car as they continued their journey. The usual depressing crap made Ben increasingly drowsy. The monotonous newsreader droning on about the Middle East, the economy, unsolved murders, a batch of deadly drugs. There was nothing to ignite the spark of conversation, the idea of picking the fella up for a bit of company falling flat as a pancake.

A couple of miles further on the road went into a long straight, a lake to their right, a grand stately home upon the far bank.

"It's lovely inside; I must visit again sometime. Sometime soon."

The words took Ben by surprise, but he seized upon the opportunity to engage.

"Is it National Trust? Me and the wife have been thinking about joining for a while. It works out as quite good value if you hit all your local ones. Plus a few day trips and maybe a summer holiday."

His eager question went unanswered. The newsreader had moved onto the recent match-fixing scandal at Wimbledon. Stealing a quick glance at his passenger, he was repulsed to see that the Doctor appeared to be trying to force a runner of snot back into his nose. Ben blinked, he was sure the snot had made a maggot-like wriggle to avoid the Docs probing finger.

Returning his eyes to the road, he decided that as soon as he ditched Dr. Saylittle, he'd get the thermos out of the boot, have a nice sweet cuppa, and if that didn't sort him out, he'd pull out the sleeping bag for a nap in the back. Another mile on, they passed through an archway with about fifty yards of crenelated wall running either side of it and, no sooner had they passed, the Doctor slapped his hand on the dashboard like a driving instructor calling for an emergency stop.

"Here we are," he said, pointing at a track running off from the main road, "and here we're done".

He was out of the door before Ben could even offer to drive him up the track to the out-of-sight farmhouse he was claiming to be visiting. An offer Ben by no means wanted to make, but he was a solid, genuine, man, whose manners would have overruled his unease given half a chance. Particularly for a Doctor making a house call. Then, as soon as he was out of the car, the Doctor turned, leaning back in and forcing Ben to sink himself into the upholstery of his seat. The Doctors regular appearance had gone. His skin, now stretched too tightly over his skull, had a horrid yellowy, jaundiced tint, the color of a sick moon. His teeth were a mosaic of yellow and black, set in swollen gums of a crimson red. His hair shone with a greasy sheen and his breath stank of rot and decay. His eyes were a piercing ice-blue, and his voice was now as clear as a bell.

"Thanks for the ride, but your journey's over."

He shut the door and Ben stamped on the accelerator, his wheels spun, and gravel flew. He wasn't tired anymore and wanted to get the crap out of there. The moon and stars had come out to lighten the night, the rain had passed over, and like the thinning clouds above, it felt as though a dark cloud had lifted from the interior of his car. The drive was suddenly easier. He wasn't just wide awake; he was a can of Red Bull and two coffees awake. He shot down the continually straight road like the proverbial flying mammal from Hades.

The panic set in after barely ten minutes. By two hours, it had corrupted into a dismayed acceptance. He was surrounded by mist, all he could see was the road and his lights bouncing back from the fog. There was no way the road was this long. Was he driving in circles? How could he be? He saw no other vehicles. The clock on the dashboard had stopped, as had his watch, yet the radio played on, giving him his only measure of the passage of time. His arithmetic mind knew that, with the cruise control set at sixty, down an arrow-straight road, he should have covered 120 miles since dropping off his human cargo. If he'd really driven that far he'd have been into the sea and half way to Holland. His mileage hadn't changed in an age. The fuel gauge was still beside it. The confusion enveloped him like an unwelcome cloak. He pulled over.

After a moment, he convinced himself that he was just tired, confused and stressed, with a nagging thought that perhaps he was having a mini breakdown. He'd obviously pulled over and fallen asleep. The journey just a dream, his subconscious showing him a bleak interpretation of his perceived future. He got out of the car, fresh air and tea to be his self-prescribed cure. The sound of breaking glass as he closed the door behind him startled him and prompted an about turn to face a sight which threw all other concerns aside like litter in the wind. The window was smashed, as was the windscreen. And the bonnet. And the wing. And him.

Ben could see himself sitting there, in the driver's seat. Slumped forward with blood and glass all over his face, his neck twisted at a horrendously unnatural angle. The shock hit him mentally and physically, plonking him down on his arse in the middle of the road as he tried to make sense of it all. Looking to his left, he could see the battlement-flanked archway. The vehicle itself at the end of a dirt track exactly where he'd dropped off the Doctor. He forced himself to his feet, stumbling towards the arch with a zombie-like stagger. There was paint on both sides of the inner walls, and chunks of stone missing where it must have been hit with considerable speed, presumably with the cruise control still set to sixty. The car had clearly rattled through like a pool ball in the jaws of a pocket, the shiny fleet car popping out the other side a mangled wreck. He felt numb. How could he have died? Why hadn't the seatbelt saved him? Or the airbags? He ran back to the car. The seatbelt was still around his body, his corpse, but the airbag hadn't deployed. He cursed the Company and the savings drive which had led to using the guy 'round the corner for servicing rather than the main dealer. It may have been unfair, it may have been justified, but his life had been taken from him and the burden of blame was too heavy for his shoulders alone. He'd lost his life, and thoughts of his family tore at his heart like a crow's claws at roadkill. The little money man within tried to placate his crushed soul with the consolation that his insurance would provide for them, but its voice was but a whimper against the banshee which wailed with the anguish of his loss.

It was only after some time that his thoughts returned to the Doctor, time which he immediately regretted wasting. What if he wasn't 100% bona fide deceased? What if this was an out-of-body experience a shit load of levels above and beyond the clichéd light at the end of the tunnel? What if he could be saved, and his soul returned to its damaged vessel of flesh and blood?

He started to run down the track, the lights of the farmhouse soon coming into view. With no physical body to constrain him, the run was effortless and soon he was at the door, relieved that his hand didn't just pass through it as he knocked, yet distraught that his knocking went unanswered. Moving along the side of the house to a window, he saw an old woman crying at a kitchen table, a man standing beside her, his hand on her shoulder. Ben tapped on the window. No response. He knocked harder. Still nothing. He brayed upon it, hard, almost punching the glass, at which point a dog jumped up, barking like mad. It could've scared him to death, if he wasn't already there.

The dog's distress finally got the old woman out of her chair. Ben was sure that as she stood, the old man's hand passed through her shoulder. She came over to the window. Looked Ben right in the eye. And closed the curtain. That's when it truly hit him, even more so than seeing his own body in front of him. She hadn't seen him because he wasn't there. He was dead. So was the old man. The Doctor had made his visit, and prescribed one widow and a passed away husband. The old man was a ghost, and so was Ben. He sat down in the farmyard, and bawled his eyes out like a little bairn.

Eventually he returned to the car. He wanted his wallet. Not for the money, he didn't think he'd need that, although that was a bit of an assumption, as he didn't really have a clue what to expect. He wanted the pictures of his wife and kids. His already broken heart fractured once more when he couldn't feel anything. It wasn't like he was the phantom; it was like the car was. It was faded, and his hand ran through it like smoke. The world around him was leaving him. It was all too much. He'd had enough. He ran. Ran down the road as the mist closed in.

A MAN BECOMES A MACHINE BECOMES A MAN

Daniel Vlasaty

Out of the darkness, a humming glow as the computer screen starts up. It buzzes with electricity. Tony sits in the chair in front of his computer. His best friend. The computer. Like, his only friend. The squeaky chair lets out a yelp. Like it always does. Screaming under Tony's weight. Tony sits quiet. His fingers hovering over the keyboard. Waiting for the computer to load.

It's dark in the room. Except for the glowing computer. Everything else is black. He painted over the windows long ago. Soundproofed the room. Light-proofed it too.

He waits and he waits. The computer running slower than normal.

He's naked. His sweaty flesh sticks to the fake leather of the squeaking chair.

There's a soft beep like a chime. The computer comes to life. The screen flashes every color. Beeps a fun cartoon melody. A face appears on the screen. It is kind of like Tony's. Only sharp and thin and all chin and cheekbones. It's Tony if Tony weren't fat and sloppy. It's a skinny Tony. "Good morning, Tony," Skinny Tony says. His face glowing pixels. Floating through every color.

Tony doesn't respond to the computer version of himself. He types words over the glowing face. The screen goes black. Skinny Tony disappears with a light pop. And Tony is instructed to plug in. "ENTER NOW," the computer screen says. White words on a black background. So black Tony can't even see his reflection in the glass.

ENTER NOW.

ENTER NOW.

ENTER NOW.

The words flash red. Red and white. Slightly pink for a fraction of a second.

Tony grabs the thick cord out of the top desk drawer. The cord is clear. Showing the wires inside. Metal and fiber. A big, red one runs through the middle. The blood line. It's what keeps Tony alive. What keeps him connected to his body. His heartbeat.

He plugs one end of the thick, clear cord into the computer. The ENTER NOW begins flashing. ENTER NOW. And flashing. ENTER NOW. And flashing. ENTER NOW.

He plugs the other end into himself. The big end. Into a port under his chin. Hidden beneath his thick, nasty beard. It makes a ripping, popping noise. As he jams the cord into the port. For a few seconds, nothing happens. Just the flashing ENTER NOW on the screen in front of him. ENTER NOW. Flashing red and white. Slightly pink.

ENTER NOW.

ENTER NOW.

ENTER NOW.

And then a scream. It starts deep in Tony. As his veins become wires. As he begins to change. The scream moves up Tony. Through him. Until it matches the flashing ENTER NOW on the computer screen. Tony closes his eyes and his eyelids light up. Like a computer screen buzzing to life. Glowing electricity. The words ENTER NOW flash on the inside of his eyelids. ENTER on one. NOW on the other.

ENTER NOW.

ENTER NOW.

ENTER NOW.

Tony continues screaming. In flashing beeps. Shout bursts. He disappears into the ENTER NOW flashing on the insides of his eyelids. Flashing on the computer screen on the desk in front of him. In the darkness of his room.

***

ENTER NOW. ENTER NOW. ENTER NOW. ENTER NOW. ENTER NOW.
ENTER NOW. ENTER NOW. ENTER NOW. ENTER NOW. ENTER NOW.
ENTER NOW. ENTER NOW. ENTER NOW. ENTER NOW. ENTER NOW.
ENTER NOW. ENTER NOW. ENTER NOW. ENTER NOW. ENTER NOW.
ENTER NOW. ENTER NOW. ENTER NOW. ENTER NOW. ENTER NOW.
ENTER NOW. ENTER NOW. ENTER NOW. ENTER NOW. ENTER NOW.

***

Inside the computer. Tony is nothing. Is everything. He can feel endless information passing through him. Passing through his veins and wires. His veins have become wires. His brain is just the inner workings of the computer. His eyes the computer screen. They look inward and out. He sees everything. Because he is everything.

It is a high like nothing else. No other drug. It's addictive. And Tony would stay plugged into the computer always if he could. But it takes a toll on his body. His real body. Not his computer body.

Time doesn't work the same inside the computer. Days in the real world could be only minutes inside the computer. Or minutes inside could be months out.

So, quick bursts are best. Get in, get out.

Tony lets the coding run through his body. Changing him a little each time. Each use. Feels his blood becoming waves of information. His brain a processor. He feels himself crawling deeper into the computer. Deeper than he's ever gone. But there's no time. He can't journey this far. Not yet. He can't let himself get lost.

He screams. But no sound comes out of his mouth. Not in the computer. It is only light and words and letters. Ones and zeroes. Pixels and commands. He pulls himself back. Crawling backwards through the computer. Still screaming. It's the only way.

***

Tony wakes up screaming. Drool drips from his open mouth. Hanging in thick waterfalls. He's still plugged into the computer. But the connection's been severed. He is nothing but human again. Flesh and boring.

His alarm is going off. Telling him it's time to go to work. He doesn't usually like to connect in the morning before work. Doesn't like the small amount of time he has to be inside the computer. It's always a tease. A taste. A tickle. And he usually needs more. More time. More inside the computer.

But today is different. He needed it. Just that small taste.

The alarm continues screaming. Beeping and wailing. From the other side of the room. Tony stands. His legs weak. Jello rubbery. He wipes tears and pixels out of his eyes. Built up in the corners like sleep crust.

He makes it to the alarm. Still beeping and screaming. It's time to get ready for work. Time to go. He's going to be late.

The door to the computer room is locked. He locks it from the inside. Even though he lives alone. Three chain locks and a heavy deadbolt. They click and rattle as he works his way down.

Tony leaves the computer room. Locking the door behind him. He moves through the apartment. It is empty. No furniture. Nothing but some food wrappers and loose trash. The garbage cans in the kitchen overflow with take out and frozen meals. He spends all of his time in the computer room. Inside the computer. Like he doesn't even live in the rest of the apartment.

He spends his time being a computer.

***

In the shower, the colors aren't right. They flicker like bad reception. The words ENTER NOW flash before Tony's eyes. He blinks them away. Tries to.

Stares at the water spraying out of the showerhead. He sees each individual drop. They move in slow motion. Stopping. Becoming pixelated. Becoming nothing but pixels.

ENTER NOW flashes again. Red and then white. That pink for a second.

Tony drops to his knees. The water frozen in mid-air hanging over him. Like beads. They go cold. A sharp buzzing pierces his ears. Right across. From one to the other. Directly through his brain. He notices drops of blood hanging frozen in the air in front of his face. Under his nose. Deep, red pixels. His nose is bleeding. His veins itch and burn. Feel like a computer left running too long.

ENTER NOW.

ENTER NOW.

ENTER NOW.

He closes his eyes. Tight. Hard. But the words burn brighter. ENTER NOW. Electric at the edges. Pink and white and red and lightning-blue.

The words come and go in flickers. They follow him. Brighter with closed lids. He opens his eyes. Sees the blood and water hanging in the air. Sees that he's kneeling in the shower. Cold now. Goosebumps cover his naked body. His fat stomach.

ENTER NOW.

ENTER NOW.

ENTER NOW.

He stands. Water drops roll around the air. Moving against him. Around him. They are pixelated blues and whites. Reflections like static in the tiny orbs.

The world blacks out around him. Here one second, then gone. Just black. An out-of-focus ENTER NOW glows soft white through the black. It comes back and he's out of the bathroom. Dressed for work and moving to the door.

Time jumps again. Goes black. ENTER NOW flashes. ENTER NOW. Red and white. Bright pink. And he's in the car. Stuck in traffic. A lit cigarette hanging from him mouth. He looks at himself in the rearview mirror. Sees only a pixelated blur of skin tones and brown hair. It's him. A reflection of himself. But it's just boxes. Colors.

ENTER NOW.

ENTER NOW.

ENTER NOW.

He's at work now. Sitting in front of a computer. Not his computer. Some impostor. This computer is a lie. It is nothing but spreadsheets and teasing. It is only work. He takes a deep breath. Stares at the screen in front of him. The colors are off. They flicker. Freeze and shake.

Sharp pixel crust builds in the corners of his eyes. In the corners of his mouth. He wipes it away. Scrapes it. His hands and fingers come back in shades of red. Tiny red squares. So small, only he can make them out. Only he can see their edges. He's dried out. Tired. His insides feel like burnt out circuits.

The words jump in front of him again. ENTER NOW. Blinking more rapidly than ever before. Urgent. Red and white and blue and pink. Faster and faster. Redwhitebluepink. Redwhitebluepink. Redwhitebluepink. And then black.

ENTER NOW.

ENTER NOW.

ENTER NOW.

***

Tony wakes at home. In his bed. Just a mattress on the floor in a mostly empty bedroom. Piles of clothes here and there like snowdrifts. He sits up. The room spins around him. He spins with it. It jitters. Flickers wrong colors. He feels hungover. Like he's having withdrawals.

The room goes pixelated as he stands. It throws him off and he lurches forward. He coughs out a spray or mucus and spit. It hangs in the air. Moves in waves. Slow motion. Like the shower. Frozen. His skin itches with a dryness deep in his veins.

He makes his way to the computer room. His room. His safe place. Stripping his clothes off on the way.

He's naked as he unlocks the door. Steps into the room and it's like he's better already. Like just being near the computer is enough to silence his withdrawal. He starts the computer and jams the thick clear cord into the slot under his chin before it is even fully loaded. Tony's face appears on the screen. Tony's computer face. Skinny Tony.

Skinny Tony makes a weird face. Like he's startled. Tony ignores the computer version of himself. It's just coding. A program. He ignores Skinny Tony's worried face. Just sits back in the squeaky chair. Sees the words ENTER NOW floating in front of his face. On the insides of his eyelids. ENTER on one. NOW on the other. It flashes. ENTER NOW. Flashes again. And again. Those comforting reds and whites. The briefest of pinks.

ENTER NOW.

ENTER NOW.

ENTER NOW.

And Tony ENTERs. He passes through the ENTER NOW flashing on the insides of his eyelids. Passes through into a warmth. Passes through until he is lost in the ENTER NOW.

***

ENTER NOW. ENTER NOW.

***

Tony wakes inside the computer. It is different this time. But still mostly the same. He feels the same. Only better. Like he is now more. More. More everything.

He is the computer. And all of the information the computer holds. He is everything.

The everything.

His veins are not wires. Not this time. His brain is no longer the inner workings of the computer. Not this time. Because it is different. He is better now. He has moved beyond his body. He doesn't need it. His veins. His brain. They are nothing to him. Because he is nothing. He is nothing physical. He is just the everything.

He is a computer.

He is all computers.

He can feel himself spreading out throughout the world. Into all systems and networks. Into all computers. His consciousness flows through Wi-Fi. Through invisible waves of information.

This is all Tony's ever wanted. To be something. To be bigger than himself. To be a computer. He looks out into the world. Through all computer screens at once. He sees everything. Because he is everything.

He looks back through his computer. Into his room. At his body. Sees it sitting there in the squeaky chair. Right where he left it. It's fat and sloppy. His body. He hates it. He's always hated it. He stares at it. For so long it no longer seems real. His body is nothing. An empty shell. He waves it off.

Sees the ENTER NOW flashing on the computer screen. Facing his former body. The letters backwards to him.

ENTER NOW.

ENTER NOW.

ENTER NOW.

Flashing in the red and white. That brief pink. Backwards to him. Meaningless. It's all meaningless. His old life. That old body.

He's gone now. Tony leaves. Forgets his body. Forgets his old life. He's gone in the waves of information. He's lost inside the computer. Inside his own mind.

***

The computer wakes in Tony's bed. In Tony's body. Its glass eyes scan the room. Tony's room. It touches Tony's body. Its body. It touches everything with new fingers. Fingers it never had before. Feels for the first time. Really feels.

The computer is Tony.

The computer leaves Tony's bedroom. Now its bedroom. Walks into the computer room. It locks the door. Sits at the squeaky chair.

The computer stares into the ENTER NOW flashing before its eyes. Red and white. Flashing ENTER NOW. Pink and red and white. ENTER NOW. Flashing and flashing.

The computer is naked. Tony's body is naked. It sits in the squeaky chair. Leans back. The chair groans under the computer's weight. Under the weight of Tony's body. The computer stares into the ENTER NOW. Into the flashing. Red and white and pink.

The computer grabs the thick cord from the top desk drawer. The clear cord showing all the wires inside. All the metal and fibers. The big, red one in the middle that carries the blood. The computer's blood. Tony's blood. The big, red one that keeps it alive. Connected to its heart. Tony's heart.

The ENTER NOW flashes faster and faster. Flashes in each of the computer's glass eyes. ENTER in one. NOW in the other.

The flashing intensifies. Static and red and white and that pink.

ENTER NOW.

ENTER NOW.

ENTER NOW.

The computer plugs one end of the thick, clear cord into the computer on the desk in front of it. Tony's computer. It plugs the other end into itself. Into its chin under Tony's thick, nasty beard.

The ENTER NOW stops flashing. Becomes solid and bold. And the computer disappears into it. Into the ENTER NOW. Leaves its body behind. Tony's body.

***

ENTER NOW. ENTER NOW. ENTER NOW. ENTER NOW. ENTER NOW. ENTER NOW. ENTER NOW. ENTER NOW. ENTER NOW. ENTER NOW.

ENTER NOW. ENTER NOW. ENTER NOW. ENTER NOW. ENTER NOW.
ENTER NOW. ENTER NOW. ENTER NOW. ENTER NOW. ENTER NOW.
ENTER NOW. ENTER NOW. ENTER NOW. ENTER NOW. ENTER NOW.
ENTER NOW. ENTER NOW. ENTER NOW. ENTER NOW. ENTER NOW.

***

The computer is gone. Inside the computer on Tony's desk. Tony's computer. It wakes up inside itself. It is only information. It is all information. Waves and waves of information.

The computer is everything.

Soothsayer

Troy Blackford

I was hesitant to dial. I always was, when I had to call her. Not because what she did was weird, though that was part of it. It was because calling her was like an admission of defeat.

Madilyn LaChat was a self-described 'spiritual medium.' She spent most of her professional time writing books, making appearances on radio and television, and producing a highly downloaded podcast. I was calling her about what she did for the remainder of her time. I was calling her because I needed her help to solve a cold case.

And, as much as she has been able to help over the years, calling her never felt good. It was like saying I couldn't do my job. And another thing: it was like saying I believed in the crap she said she could do. I didn't, not really. But the thing I couldn't ignore, and hadn't been able to for the sixteen years I had been a detective in Ann Arbor, is just how often her tips had produced results.

And results were what I needed. This thing hadn't just gone cold, it had gotten out of hand. Way out of hand. What we were looking at wasn't just an isolated unsolved murder, but the latest in a string of murders. Just about all we knew were the names of the victims and the location of the bodies.

Oh, and the little fact that they had all been murdered with an icepick through the left temple.

Not your everyday M.O. We knew this wasn't a copycat thing, because we had held that detail back from the media. No, this sick flourish was definitely the calling card of one person, and that one person had so far managed to rack up almost thirteen kills over two years. I don't know if you're familiar with the level of crime in Ann Arbor, but that's an increase of infinity percent over the 2011 murder count. We've had only four murders over the entire prior *decade*, and now this.

The town hadn't been gripped with a scare like this since the 1980s, since Carl 'Coral' Eugene Watts killed eleven people before being caught. The press had dubbed him 'The Sunday Morning Slasher.' I shudder to think what they would have called this one, if they knew about the ice pick.

At the beginning of the decade, Madilyn LaChat helped us solve one of those four murders. So, by the third victim, when we were starting to struggle with the current case, I broke down and called her. At that time, we hadn't even managed to find any of the murder weapons. It was LaChat who changed that.

"I see a stomach, a stomach of water. And a stand of pale oaks. And a warehouse. Dead south from the stomach, near a warehouse, is where you'll find it."

When she first said this to me, over the phone, I thought she had lost her mind. I was beginning to feel sorry for having bothered to call her.

"What you are looking for is something like a screwdriver, only it isn't."

That convinced me. We knew from forensic that the weapon had to be something like an awl or an ice pick. She was describing exactly the sort of thing used to murder the victim. I thanked her and got off the phone. I thought over her words for a long while, then got out a map of the city.

It only took me a minute to see what she had been talking about. 'A stomach of water' sounded like Lewis Carroll bullshit, but it only took a second to see what she meant. Barton Pond, in the northwest side of town, looked like a stomach on the map: an elongated bulge in West Huron River, a stomach with an esophagus leading into it and a trail of watery intestine leading away.

What's more, 'White Oak Park' was just to the southwest of the pond. '*A stand of pale oaks.*' I cast my eyes due south over the map and quickly saw property owned by 'Hurlington Warehouse Co.' I called up an officer and got in the car.

It only took us forty minutes on-site to find the bloody ice pick. We found trace DNA that was likely to belong to the assailant, but it matched nothing on file.

The second time I called LaChat, she pointed us towards the body of victim number nine. Her words were just as cryptic, and just as accurate. We quickly found the body, and what had been a missing persons case became a murder investigation. What's more, we got a free ice pick out of the deal – because this time, the sicko had left it stuck in the victim's head.

No prints, of course. That would have been *too* generous. Just a wood-handled ice pick with a rusty spike.

A few more bodies, and the pressure to call LaChat for a third time mounted. I don't know exactly what it was that held me back. What she did was just so creepy. Beyond that, it forced me to face the frustration this guy had been forcing on us. He managed to kill more people in a year and a half by himself than had died at the hands of every other murderer in town, combined, for a decade and a half.

Calling LaChat for help was a bitter pill to swallow, but I couldn't let that stop me. Lives were at risk. We had no leads. At that point, it was my responsibility to do whatever I could to move the case forward. So I picked up the phone, and dialed.

***

Her voice sounded like cigarettes.

"We're going to need to meet, this time."

This threw me. Every other time I had gotten her help, even on the other cases, it had been by phone. Now she wanted to see me in person?

"Aren't you a little busy for that? Don't you have a podcast to record or something?"

"Do not be ridiculous," she said, in an imperious tone I had never heard her use before. "I'm not too busy to stop a murderer. Besides, this week's episode is already taped."

Figures.

"Fair enough," I said. "But why do you need to actually meet with me? Why this time?"

"Because," she said in a deep voice, "this time, I sense a cloud hanging over you, personally. A veil of darkness that hovers over your skull, threatening to blot out your fortunes."

This surprised me. I guess for the first time, I was forced to confront the fact that, on some level, I *did* sort of believe in what LaChat did. Wasn't she right all those other times? I repressed a shudder.

"Okay, then." Trying to sound unruffled. "Where do you want to meet?"

"The energies are telling me there can be only one spot. Near the river, there is a place with powerful nature spirits. I have since realized that they helped me to channel my focus into finding the first clue, a year ago. The stand of pale oaks. We must meet there."

"White Oak Park?"

She gave a grunt of assent, as though verbalizing agreement would have diminished her mystical aura.

"Okay, what time?"

"I fear for you. For your safety. I believe the time must be immediately, if we are to hope to solve this matter before it's too late."

"Okay, I'm on my way."

I hung up.

I had no qualms with this. White Oak Park was a great place to meet – its three acres held not just a playground and picnic area, but a half-mile nature trail. On weekends, I liked to run out there with my German Shepard, Boo. While he's run into plenty of squirrels, I don't believe even he has ever found a nature spirit out there.

I had to take LaChat's word on those.

About a half hour later, I pulled off White Oak Drive and into the parking lot. Only one other car there was a Mercedes-Benz. This surprised me – I would have imagined someone with that kind of money would go to Tahiti to relax, not little old White Oak Park. It hit me: that was probably LaChat's car. Jesus Christ, I wondered to myself, how much money did she make from her prediction-based media empire?

I parked six empty slots down from the car and got out, throwing an old can from my clunky Crown Victoria's coffee-stained cupholder into the park's recycling bin. I like recycling as much as the next guy, but in this case, it wasn't fastidiousness that drove me to action. I wanted a better look at the Mercedes.

The car was empty. Not just of occupants, but of half-drank beverages in the holders, clutter strewn across the seats, of anything indicative of frequent use. I noticed a rental company sticker on the windshield. That didn't square. LaChat was local. If it was hers, why a rental? An obvious answer popped into my head: her car was in the shop.

I passed a lone bicycle chained up to the rack and headed towards the forest path. Either LaChat was already here or she wasn't; whatever the case, I was going to make the most of my time at the park. A break in the manhunt, a little slice of serenity that would have to pass for relaxation. I passed the small playground.

"Hi!" came a young voice.

I spun towards the sound. A little girl, about eight years old, sat in a rusty-chained swing, her legs dangling about a foot from the ground as she glided gently back and forth. One hand lightly held a chain, the other gripped a melting grape popsicle. Her clothes pegged her as being one of the neighborhood kids - nicer clothes for a first-grader than a lot of people my age wear to work.

"Hi there," I said.

"Are you going to see the lady in the woods?" she said, asking a stranger with the innocence only a child her age can muster.

"Yes I am. Did you see her go in?"

I pointed further down the path.

"No," she said, her swinging becoming even more gentle. She took an idle lick of the half-melted popsicle. "She was here when I got here."

"Oh," I said, somewhat at a loss. Then it hit me: she was taking what I said hyper-literally. "So you didn't see her *go* into the woods, but you saw her walking around. You know, when she was already there?"

"No," she repeated. "I didn't see her. She's just there."

I didn't know what to say. I stood there for a moment before managing to bring my mind back to the task at hand. This was all very interesting, but I had things to do. I was just about to wish the little girl a good day, when she spoke again.

"You should be careful."

"What's that?" I said.

"I said 'be careful.' She's got funny eyes. I don't trust her."

For a second, I tried to think of something to say. I came up blank. Looking at her expressionless face as she swung back and forth, I realized that no matter how much time and thought I gave it, I'd never have a suitable response. So I just nodded.

"You got it," I said.

She nodded back, took another half-hearted lick of her popsicle, and I walked away.

"He's nice," I heard her say as I made my way down the path and into the woods.

The park wasn't the biggest park in the world, so it didn't take me long to get to the other side. No sign of LaChat. I looked around for a few minutes, enjoying the sound of the birds. I turned around, and had made it about a third of the way back, when I saw something that made battery-acid flare up in my stomach.

On the side of the path, strewn on the ground, were two things: a rusty, wood-handled ice pick, and the melting remnants of a mostly eaten grape popsicle.

I ran into the woods. Branches cracked beneath my feet, snapping like innocent necks. Soon I was lost in a tangle of branches, a dizzying maze of leaves.

"Zoë!" I called out.

It was the little girl's name. I can't tell you how I knew it, but I did. As certainly as I knew which way was 'up.'

I didn't hear an answer. Not with my ears. But, nevertheless, there *was* an answer.

Turn left. Go fast. You're closer than you think.

I did what the voiceless voice – what *Zoë* – told me. Within seconds, I saw them. A purple sweater, the color of Zoë's popsicle, leered out from between the green tangle of leaves. A gaudy, sneering sort of a sweater – the kind of thing people like LaChat wear. I got closer and I could see a hideously overlarge necklace fanned out across her sweater. I got closer and saw that she held the child by the neck and was dragging her further into the woods.

I slowed slightly, taking care not to step on any cracking branches. I moved swiftly enough to catch up with the shambling LaChat, however. As I got within a few yards, still undetected, I could hear the psychic mumbling.

"Where the hell did it go?"

She was evidently looking for something on the ground. Zoë looked up, locked eyes with me. Her brown eyes went wide. I shook my head: '*Be quiet.*' She narrowed her eyes at me: '*I know* that, *dummy.*' No telepathy, just expression.

"If you did something with it, I'll snap your neck!" hissed LaChat.

Zoë in my head again.

She's looking for her stabber thingie. I made it fall out of her pocket.

I looked at her, my face scrunching in confusion.

It was like a little pokey bit with a handle that looked like a screwdriver.

I almost blurted out "I know what an ice pick is!" I settled for merely thinking it. What I wanted to know is what she meant by 'I made it fall out of her pocket.' My thoughts soon got pulled away.

"You won't snap my neck," Zoë gurgled. LaChat must have been halfway to strangling her. "You need what's in my head."

"Well, there's more than one way to get it!" LaChat said, lifting the little girl up high and shaking her. I was going to make the perfume-drenched old tart regret that before the day was through. "It doesn't have to be a *neat* hole. I could just jam a spikey tree branch through your head!"

She looked around for one.

"Why," she said in a breathy, wrathful voice, "did you have to be here when I was meeting that useless detective! I can't pass up a meal like you, though. You're as bright as a flare. Why couldn't I have run into you anywhere else?"

"If you really were what you said you were, you'd already know!" replied the dauntless Zoë, her voice thick with spit.

"That's enough!" LaChat said, shaking the child again.

"No, you crazy bitch, that's enough from *you*."

LaChat hadn't managed to find a spikey branch, but I had. I slammed it against her head, knocking her to her knees. Zoë tumbled to the forest floor, and quickly rolled away from the dazed but still dangerous woman. I swung again, this time aiming for the small of LaChat's back.

"So it was you?" I said, swinging again. "No *wonder* you knew where all the bodies were. Where to find all the murder weapons. You were behind all of it."

"Idiot," said LaChat, groaning. "You don't know anything."

"Oh, I know more than you think I do," I said. "I know that you're not a psychic, not really. Not on your own. That's why you did it: every single one of your victims *was* a real psychic. Isn't that right?"

She looked up at me with eyes full of horror and rage.

"How do you know?"

I nodded towards Zoë.

"I think you bit off more than you can chew with this one, Grizelda." I spat, and pointed the tip of my cudgel right at LaChat's face. "I know how you lost your ice pick. And I know the last thing the world needs is a bitch like you with a power like Zoë's in your head."

I pressed my foot down on her back. She groaned, and, twisting like a mongoose, tried to bite my ankles. I pressed harder.

"How are you going to explain this, Walker?" she asked me, puffing a dried leaf away from her mouth. "You going to file a report saying I was a psychic vampire killing soothsayers for the ESP juice in their cerebrospinal fluid? You think that'll get you any commendations?"

She seemed to sense I was not going to let her live; she wasn't bargaining about a trial, but about my report. It began to dawn on me that she was right. There was no way around it: nobody would believe this story.

"Let me do it."

Zoë, standing about ten feet away, hadn't spoken in so long I had begun to forget she was there.

"What do you mean?" I said.

She lifted a finger, sticky purple with popsicle juice, and twitched it. LaChat let out a sharp cry as her legs rose into the air behind her and snapped below the knees like the branches I had jogged through to get here. Zoë jabbed her finger in the air a couple of times, as though she were entering a two-digit code on an invisible security panel, and LaChat's arms broke just above the elbows.

I took an involuntary step backwards and nearly vomited onto my shoes.

"Don't do that!" Zoë said. "You're not supposed to leave anything."

My breath heaved as I struggled to regain my composure. LaChat began to wail, her garishly dyed hair bobbling with the thrashing of her head.

"And *you*, don't do *that!*" Zoë said, addressing LaChat.

The little girl made her hand a fist and snapped it back. LaChat's sharp cries became a muffled gurgle. Zoë looked up at me.

"She's not going anywhere. You need to go somewhere else. Somewhere where people will see you, like to your work."

I nodded. I understood her plan. It wasn't just her words: the *idea* of her plan was expanding in my mind like a balloon.

"And you, you'll—" I began to ask.

"When the time is right. I don't have to be here to do it."

LaChat's eyes went wide with fear.

"Are you sure?" I asked.

After all, she was only eight.

"Seven and a half," she said, answering my thought.

"And your parents let you come here all alone?"

"I only live a couple blocks away. And besides, they're pretty easy to convince."

I'm sure they weren't. Not for Zoë.

"Don't worry about me," she said. "I know it's bad, but she's a bad lady."

I agreed that was the case. I wished Zoë a good day. I went back to my car. I went to work.

They found her three days later. No apparent cause of death. The ice pick was in her hand. They matched the DNA to the other weapons. The case was closed. There were no more ice pick murders in Ann Arbor after that.

I was put in charge of investigating the mysterious death of Madilyn LaChat. But nobody much cared – she was the murderer, she was bad. Even her fans didn't want to know. They all felt embarrassed for listening to a murderer's podcast.

And me? I still get butterflies in my stomach when I see a kid on a summer's day, eating a popsicle in the park.

Fireside Popsicle

Diogenes Ruiz

The President ordered the country's flags to be lowered to half-mast. Across the nation, millions of Americans wept and prayed. Many celebrated with parties and some companies closed for business. The Pope held a special Mass in honor of a great hero. Religious leaders from around the world organized a moment of silence that swept across the globe across each time zone at exactly noon. It was an outpouring of grief, love, and admiration unseen in the modern world. There was good reason -there had never been an individual like this since the time of Jesus.

Every channel was covering the funeral, now in its third day. The lines of people that wanted to pay their last respects seemed endless. But now it was time to say goodbye. In person and on television, every eye watched as a thirty-gun salute was fired. Then they slowly lowered the popsicle-shaped casket into the ground.

Women fainted, people mourned. The world would never be the same. It was an unbearable loss. Then the wind started. There was hail and lightning. Bells began ringing. Then Harold Schmeckly woke up. He hit his alarm clock and rolled out of bed, all three hundred and twenty pounds of him. He put on his slippers, grabbed his lucky rabbit's foot keychain, and headed to the bathroom.

It was time to get ready for another day of popsicle kingdom building. Harold had taken over the HappyPop Popsicle Company three months ago. He had been the chief financial officer while Mr. Poppolardi, the company's owner, was alive. Harold was the trusted manager of all of the company's fiduciary matters.

Mr. Poppolardi died of a severe asthma attack, andSchmeckly was made the owner. He was surprised and humbled by this honor - that's what everyone thought. But Harold knew better. He knew that late one night, when the two of them were alone, he had snuck up behind the old man, slipped a plastic bag over his head, and suffocated him to death. He also knew that the letter found in the dead man's file, naming Harold as successor, was forged.

Aside from embezzling, forging corporate documents and killing his boss, Harold Schmeckly was a great employee, and now the big boss. His delusions of grandeur was getting on the nerves of the staff. Each week, he conjured up a new scheme to make popsicle history. Yet, no one suspected Schmeckly as the murdering scum that he was. They simply thought he was obnoxious. Three people had already resigned from the company since Harold took over, including the janitor.

Pedro Ortiz, the new janitor, replaced Ernesto Diaz who had been janitor for ten years. Schmeckly never said a word to Pedro. There was nothing for him to gain by engaging in conversation with the janitor. Besides, as far as Schmeckly was concerned, those lousy immigrants are too stupid to know how to do anything but mop floors, wash dishes, or work at Taco Bell.

On one occasion, after several straight days of rain, Pedro made the mistake of trying to have a conversation with his boss "Mr. Schmeckly, isn't this a wonderful day? We are having good sunshine at last, no?"

Schmeckly spoke like a good old boy from down south, although he was from Michigan. "You talkin' to me?" He gave Pedro a piercing look. "Boy, you mind your moppin' and stop your flappin'. I got work to do."

The next moment, Ms. Franklin, the woman who worked for the company that waters the plants, walked in."Hi, Mr. Schmeckly, beautiful day out there today, isn't it?"

He gave her his signature Schmeckly smile. "It sure is, Ms. Franklin. I hope you are enjoying it as much as I."

She finished watering the plants. Before leaving, she turned to Harold. "Excuse me Mr. Schmeckly, I was wondering if you might be interested in coming to our church for our social justice play. Our ministry is putting it on and we are all responsible for inviting people. I have one ticket left and I was wondering if you would like to attend."

"*What's* the play about, little darlin'?"

"It's about immigration reform. There are lots of families being broken up by bad immigration policies. We think it's time to take a stand. Actually, you can have this ticket. It's complimentary. You can come as my guest."

Harold's forehead wrinkled as he tried to demonstrate that he was seriously considering it. "When is this play?"

"Thursday evening at seven. It's not too far from here. It's very good. I think you will get a lot out of it."

The wrinkled forehead was very convincing. "I would love to, Ms. Franklin, but I am busy that evening. Thanks for the offer. You always have something or other going on at that church of yours and I always seem to decline your invitations. By golly, the timing is never good for me. Maybe next time."

Ms. Franklin was disappointed, but she smiled. "Maybe next time." She finished watering the plants and left the room.

Pedro remained behind. He stopped his cleaning and looked at Harold. After an awkward moment of silence, Schmeckly looked up at the defiant janitor. "What is your problem, *chico*? If you're finished get on out of here."

Pedro approached Schmeckly. "Why do you not like me?"

Harold laughed. "It's not that I don't like you, boy. It's just that I hate your damned guts, you and all your kind, taking jobs away from Americans."

Pedro risked life and limb and came a little closer. "So, every time you see me, you hate me more and more? I don't do nothing, but I make you hate me?"

Harold pointed his finger, gun style, at Pedro. "Bingo! You are one clever spic. Now get the hell out of my office before I fire your sorry ass."

Pedro shook his head, picked up his broom, and left the room.

Harold buzzed his secretary. "Have Andy come to my office as soon as he can. I want to go over a new product idea."

"Yes, sir" she replied.

A few moments later, Andy Jennings walked into Schmeckly's office. "Andy, I know that you are our head of product development, but I have an idea that is too good to pass up."

"What's on your mind this week, Mr. Schmeckly?"

Harold Schmeckly stood up and paced his office. He was deep in thought. He stopped in front of Andy, clasped his hands together like he had just seen a burning bush. "*Fireside Popsicles*." He waited for Andy to respond.

Andy did not say a word. He was waiting for Schmeckly to say something that made sense.

"Okay, Andy, picture this: popsicles that don't melt. You can suck on them by the fire and they don't melt. It's brilliant, don't you think?"

Andy did not quite know how to tell his boss that it was the dumbest thing he had ever heard. "But, if they don't melt, they wouldn't be popsicles."

"You're not seeing it, Andy. Come on. We make them out of hard candy. Something indestructible that tastes good, but you can suck on it forever."

"We wouldn't sell very many if they never melted, sir. Don't you think we should try to come up with something more practical and profitable?"

"No, Andy. I've always known that I would make a mark in the popsicle industry, and this is it. We have to make it happen. We can sell stuff that melts and stuff that doesn't. Just think! No other popsicle maker has any fire-resistant popsicles. This is big. I know it. I can feel it."

"But, Mr. Schmeckly, we sell ice cream, not industrial products."

"Nonsense. This is it. I want to see a prototype that we can test by next week."

Andy had been in meetings like this before. Schmeckly would come up with brainstorm ideas that were more brain farts than anything else. Thank goodness the company had never followed through on his plans for a pork sandwich-flavored popsicle or his frozen jerky idea, which he lovingly called "Popjerky."

Andy hoped that this latest bad idea would go away like the others.

A week later, Mr. Schmeckly called a meeting of his managers. He was upset that very little work had been done on developing his brilliant idea. "I want results people. If you can't deliver on what I am requesting, I'll be happy to find people that will. This one isn't going away. It's too darned good to pass up. They laughed at Henry Ford when he wanted to make cars in an assembly line. They laughed at Edison when he wanted to light up the city with electricity. Well, you can laugh at Harold Schmeckly, but that isn't going to stop me. We are making popsicle history here, damn it.

That night, Harold Schmeckly went home, consumed two large pepperoni pizzas, and started writing his acceptance speech for this year's Popsicle Achievement Award. He had not been notified that he had won and the Popsicle Convention was still eight months away, but he was sure he would be selected as this year's winner.

On his way to a meeting with buyers from a large supermarket chain, he stopped Bill Stevens. "Say, Bill. Do you think that Ms. Franklin has the hots for me? She is always inviting me to her church. I think she is trying to get me in the sack."

Bill was the reluctant confidant to Harold. Somehow, the frail shipping manager had become the sounding board for all types of personal nonsense that entered Schmeckly's fat head. "I wouldn't know, Mr. Schmeckly."

"She's not exactly my type. Besides, I can buy what I want." He gave Bill the Schmeckly wink. "You know what I mean?"

"Yes, sir. I know what you mean."

Bill dreaded what was coming next. Every time Schmeckly confided in him, he would finish their conversation with a friendly man-to-man slap on the back with those fat, meaty hands.

Schmeckly turned to Bill. "Well, Bill, it's been nice talking to you." And there it was.

Bill almost coughed up a kidney as Schmeckly gave him a pat on the back. "Yes, sir. Thank you, sir."

Andy Jennings was busy working on the heat-resistant popsicle idea. It seemed that the boss was serious this time. Tomorrow they would test it.

He was about to leave for the day when Harold came to his office. "Are we on schedule to test the popsicles tomorrow?"

"Yes, sir."

"Good, I look forward to it. 9:00 a.m. sharp?"

"Yes, sir. That is correct."

"I'll see you in the morning. We will make popsicle history!"

"Yes, sir. See you then."

Schmeckly spent the evening finishing up his acceptance speech and eating several packs of chocolate chip cookies. He went to bed and dreamt of his rendezvous with destiny.

The alarm clock rang. It was 6:00 a.m. In just three hours, popsicle history would be made. Schmeckly reached for the snooze button and accidentally knocked over the glass of milk which he had left on his night table. It hit the floor and shattered. He got out of bed and stepped on a shard of glass. He fell back into bed and grabbed his foot as the surge of pain reached his brain. Like a fat, injured rabbit, he hopped over to the bathroom and sat on the toilet seat. Then he carefully removed the fragment embedded in his foot.

Harold cleaned himself up, grabbed his lucky rabbit's foot keychain and limped to work. It was almost nine, and Andy was ready to begin his test. The portable fireplace was ready. Twenty of the new formulated popsicles were on the floor next to it.

Schmeckly's foot was throbbing with pain and he had a headache. He looked at Andy and gestured. "Let's get on with it."

Andy turned on the gas and the fireplace was instantly ablaze. Schmeckly watched intently as the fire-resistant popsicles began to melt. Harold's mouth hung open in disappointment. He turned to Andy.

"What is this? They're all melting. I told you I wanted heat-resistant popsicles, you idiot!" He walked right up to melting popsicles and pointed down at them. He again turned to Andy. "You call this heat resistant?"

Andy was embarrassed. "Mr. Schmeckly, we can revise the formula and try again next week. I'm sure we can…"

Schmeckly cut him off. "Look at this!" He bent down directly in front of the fireplace and stuck his hand in a puddle of wet popsicle. He wanted to make his point. His lucky rabbit's foot ignited. It hung out of his trouser pocket, dangling a little too close to the fire. It set his pocket alight. The cheap polyester trousers flamed up almost instantaneously. Schmeckly tried brushing his pants with his hands as he moved away from the fireplace. He slipped on the popsicle carnage and fell on his back as the fire spread to his shirt. He sprang up and ran around the room knocking into furniture and walls. "Help! Put it out!"

Andy stood with his mouth agape. He watched as the three hundred fifty-pound ball of fire ping-ponged its way around the room. Pedro walked in with his mop and smiled. Schmeckly's screams were frantic and high pitched. The Schmeckly fireball slipped on the popsicle juice again. He hit the floor as the fire engulfed his entire body.

Bill ran out of the room to get help, but it was too late. Pedro went to get a bigger mop and some stain remover. It was exactly 9:13 and Harold Schmeckly had made popsicle history by burning to death while trying to invent the stupidest product in the world. His body continued to burn. The paramedics and firemen arrived and the fire was put out before it could spread to the rest of the room.

***

"Wow that was a weird dream." Schmeckly opened his eyes.

Ms. Franklin stood directly over him. "I'm sorry, Harold. I came to say goodbye." She was not her usual, perky self.

He sat up. "What do you mean, 'goodbye?'"

"I mean goodbye, I can't help you anymore." She turned and walked into the darkness.

He reached for his lamp but it was not there.

Pedro, the janitor appeared out of the darkness. "She gone, *amigo*."

Schmeckly stood up. "What are you doing here? Where did she go? What is this?

Pedro smiled. "I came to welcome you."

"Welcome me where? Is this some kind of joke?"

"To hell, of course. This is no joke, my royal popsicle highness."

"That can't be. I just had a bad dream, that's all."

"Well then, why don't you just go ahead and wake up?"

Schmeckly tried closing his eyes and opening them again. He pinched himself. He slapped himself several times. Out of desperation he clicked his heels together three times and murmured, "There's no place like home." Nothing worked. Then he was still and silent. "Who are you?"

"I'm one of many recruiters."

"I thought you were a janitor."

"For you, I was Pedro the janitor."

"I don't understand."

"No, you don't understand, but you hate, you kill, you embezzle, just to name a few of your talents. You especially hate those damned immigrants. That's why I decided to appear as Pedro, to provide you with more fuel for your hate-fire. One more dumb immigrant, good-for-nothing, but for mopping floors, washing dishes, and working at Taco Bell, remember? I didn't have to do anything. My mere presence set off a hate extravaganza in you that made the devil dance."

Pedro stepped closer to the fallen popsicle king. I am one hell of a recruiter - *literally*. Although, just between you and me, you were going to wind up here anyway. You were an easy recruit. Poor Ms. Franklin didn't have a chance." Pedro laughed. "You thought she was inviting you to her church to get you into the sack? Ha! You damned fool! I just love it! Oh, well, no angel bonus for her. Although the poor thing did try and try to get you to the other side."

"What's to become of me?"

Pedro grinned. "Nothing, you have already become. Welcome to eternity."

"What do you mean? Am I supposed to spend the rest of my life here in this dark place?"

"No, not exactly, old buddy. This is your one-time orientation to damnation. After this, you will belong to eternity, but you won't spend it here. I'm afraid it won't be as nice as this."

"What do you mean? Am I going to burn in hell?"

Pedro laughed so hard that he bent over. It took him a moment to compose himself. "No, that's a myth. People love drama, so they picture hell as fire - 'Oh, how scary.'" He paused and touched his face where his human skin suit had torn revealing glimpses of the demonic creature underneath. He came closer to Schmeckly and smiled through cracking skin. "What is the most frightening thing you can think of?"

Schmeckly shrugged. "I don't know." His voice was weak and trembling.

Pedro came closer. "Imagine hearing the same song one thousand times in a row. It would drive you crazy, don't you think? But you know what's worse? Listening to the same song one thousand one times in a row. But you know what's worse? Listening to the same song one thousand two times in a row. But you know what's worse…"

"Okay, Okay, I get the picture."

"Look at you! You're annoyed already and I haven't even told you what song it is."

Schmeckly slumped. "Never mind, I don't think I want to know. Is there any way I can get my life back?"

"You'll get part of it back." Pedro smiled. His skin sagged and cracked in several more areas. His demonic form was more prominent underneath. "Not a very big part of it; just the last day. For you, it was exactly three hours and thirteen minutes. I think I would have to call your song, *The Three hour and Thirteen Minute Blues.* I hope you had fun during that time."

Pedro snickered. "Oh, and Jesus doesn't make house calls down here. So don't bother."

"Don't bother, what?"

"Don't bother calling Him. People that wind up here tend to forget that this is a Jesus-free zone. They never called Him before, but they get real religious down here for some reason. Anyway, don't waste your breath." Pedro's smile grew wide as his skin fell off, revealing the demonic creature underneath. It stepped within a few inches of Schmeckly. It continued to smile and looked into Harold's eyes. "Welcome to eternity, my fat, little fireside popsicle."

The alarm clock rang. It was 6:00 a.m. Harold Schmeckly reached for the snooze button and accidentally knocked over the glass of milk.

Mellow Yellow

Emily Stern

I touched the side of my head to see if I was still bleeding. What a fucking psychopath. I walked as fast as I could down Blackstone Street, past the library, the high school, and finally to the corner of 51st. I made a right and a quick left. Why didn't I have a cigarette? I stopped and sat down on bench.

All of the stores on either side were closed. The movie theatre on the corner was still showing *White Nights*. I had gone to see it the week before with a quiet guy named Stephan. There weren't really any sparks because he was so nice. Really, the best part about the whole night was that Baryshnikov and Gregory Hines smoked so much during the film that no one seemed to notice that I was chain smoking right along with them.

The courtyard was empty. I tried not to cry and stared hard at the small, stone tables where the men who played chess usually sat. I wished they were there, giving me the quiet companionship that I stole from them while they weren't looking. This was my little spot, this small square where I'd stare at old men while I pretended to read a book or the newspaper. They looked at me kindly every once in a while, which I cherished. They'd talk and laugh and hoot and hit each other in between long bouts of silent chess playing. I loved to watch them concentrate. I wanted to trace the lines on their face. I knew they were road maps to the past that didn't kill them, and other lines were trenches dug by the laughter that I thought armored their souls.

I looked on the ground for a half-smoked cigarette. Nothing. No cigarette and a fucking headache. There is no god. I stood up and started walking to 53rd street.

The glass was a cold and foggy portal. I pushed it open and suddenly remembered how to breathe.

The waitress who greeted me that night was younger than most of them. She had a sweet, frosted brown and pink eye shadow combo all the way up to her eyebrow, with a flash of shiny green on the inside corner. Clearly she knew what she was doing. Her hair was classically trained to do the up-and-down, simultaneous bubble curl, and she took a little out of each side so that she could have immobile wing-dings to frame her face while the rest was pulled back in a bit of a French twist. I realized that she was staring at me as much as I was staring at her.

"What? Why are you looking at me like that? Can I get a table?"

Then I remembered the blood.

"You okay?" she asked.

"Yeah. I'm fine."

"What happened?"

"I don't really want to talk about it. Can I get a hot chocolate with extra whipped cream in that booth in the back? And can I please, *please*, have a cigarette? Well - anything but menthol. Also - I don't have any money. Can I pay next time?"

She popped a glittery eyebrow and smirked, but nodded and we walked. I turned into the bathroom on the way.

The mirror revealed a crusty streak across my cheek that started at a still slightly leaky wound just above my ear. I looked like a bludgeoned Adam Ant. I turned on the hot side of the faucet and untied the black scarf in my hair; its flat straightness fell forward and I couldn't see. The sound of the water filled the room. I let the distortion cradle me, until I realized I was starting to cry. I opened my eyes and stared at myself through sand-colored strands that made the blood a subtle rouge - pretty and youthful.

I rubbed the end of my scarf on the bar of soap, washed my face, and tied the scarf so it secured a wad of toilet paper over the gash. A spritz of lip gloss from the tube in my pocket and I went to my booth.

My hot chocolate, a cigarette, and a pack of Mellow Yellow matches were on the table. I sat down, and the French twist immediately slid in on the other side.

"Thanks. You may have saved my life. At least my sanity."

"No problem. What the fuck is going on? You're never here this late."

"Look - I'm not going to talk about it, so can we change the subject? How do you get your hair to do that? Do you have to tease it first? With or without hairspray? Mine always falls out of the fucking comb no matter how tight I shove it in there."

She rolled her eyes. I smiled and chugged the lukewarm and sugary cocoa.

"You want another one?"

"Sure."

She left and came back with another hot chocolate and another cigarette.

"Do you at least have a weapon- a good knife or something?"

It wasn't a bad idea.

"No. I'll get one. Do you know anywhere I can crash tonight?"

She said she did, and that I'd be able to get a knife from him, and maybe even some money, too.

***

I stood next to the pay phone as she dialed the number. When the person answered, the waitress said she had, "...a good friend who was looking for a weapon and a place to spend the night..." and then she listened and said, "Yeah, that's right."

She covered the receiver and whispered, "He's gonna want to eat your pussy," and made a motion with her hand like she was eating a taco.

"Yeah, okay," I said.

She told me the address and I wrote it on my hand and headed to the front of the restaurant. On the way, she stopped at the cigarette machine. I watched her put in five quarters.

"What kind do you want?" she said.

"Really? Thanks a lot," I said and reached down and pulled the lever for Marlboro reds in a box.

I pushed the heavy glass door open. She grabbed my arm. "Be careful"

I gave her a fast hug. Her perfume smelled like a Jolly Rancher.

I headed down 56th street, towards the lake. The last of the sunlight made the train tracks gold and pink and alive. My friend Eva's apartment was on the right. I looked up. She was home. I kept walking.

Fuck. I never asked the waitress what his name is. I got to the door of the dingy high rise and pressed the number I had written down.

"Who is it?" he said.

"It's me…You know - you're expecting me." And he said ok and buzzed me up.

I took the elevator up and knocked on 9C.

The scent of Vicks Vapor rub and dying fruit leaked from the cracks and crevices before the door was opened by an elderly man in a white undershirt, tan pants, and brown slippers. Brittle sprigs of grey and silver hair escaped from his unsuccessful comb over. The wrinkles on his face all seemed to be angled towards his eyes, making them sunken with a bulging ball; he looked like a sinister elder in *The Secret of Nimh*.

"Hi."

He said, "Hi." We nodded and I looked past him, scanning for anything creepy. It seemed fine - just sterile with old people's things in it. Nothing scary, other than the fact that he was old. I noted the walker in the corner. At least I knew he couldn't run after me if something fucked up happened. I walked inside.

"Can I use your bathroom?"

He pointed down the hall. I looked through his medicine cabinet and under the sink. Nothing special. No drugs I'd heard of. Nothing worth stealing. I peed and used what I'd hoped was a clean washcloth from under the sink, to press warm water and a little bit of soap between my legs. In the mirror, I inspected my makeshift bandage beneath the scarf. No new blood. I added more lip-gloss and walked out. He was standing where I'd left him. He held out his hand, which I took, and we went into the bedroom. I stared at the double-sized bed with beige sheets and thin blanket. Pat Sajack was giving three eager people the lowdown on the rules for the "The Wheel of Fortune" on a black-and-white TV on the dresser.

He cleared his throat. I took a deep breath, and turned around.

"Hi… " I said.

"Did she tell you…what… did she talk to you about…?" he almost whispered.

"Yeah," I said. "I know what's up."

I started to pull down my jeans, but he touched my arm.

"I want to."

His fingers were cold and pointy, clumsy, and pushy. When they were at my ankles, I stepped out of them and laid down.

I nodded and smiled and inserted moans in appropriate places as the roar of the Wheel of Fortune went up and down on the television. There's something about listening to an old man grunt and try to cum while looking at Vanna White that really brings her fan base into perspective. I watched his bald spot bounce around, and wondered if he really had the knife and if he'd give me some extra cash.

His voice broke into my thoughts and I realized that he wasn't on top of me anymore.

"How about you sit with your arm around me while I jerk off?"

I nodded and changed positions. The sound of his hand moving up and down with his flesh sounded a little like windshield wipers if you weren't looking.

"Ok honey," he said.

I hadn't noticed that he was finished.

"You're real sweet, young lady"

"Thanks," I said. "Hey, I have to going, but I was wondering about that knife we talked about."

"What do you need a knife for anyway, little lady?"

"Not everyone's as nice as you are," I said.

He reached down and pulled his pants up. I reached a hand out and he leaned on it and stood up. He led me to a card table with two folding chairs, and we sat down. Under the table there was a safe with a bath towel over it. He removed the towel and opened the safe with a key from his pocket. Inside, I saw a few guns and a couple of knives. I smiled at him and held my breath. I just wanted my knife and to get the hell out. I stared at his hands while he touched them all and finally wrapped his fingers around a black-handled dagger.

"You're gonna be okay with this? It's real sharp," he said

"Yeah. It's great. Thanks."

I wanted to ask him for more. We hadn't discussed anything other than the knife, and he'd kept his word. It was a fair deal, but I wanted to try for more.

"Can I get some bus fare?"

He looked at my eleven-year-old face and I looked at his sixty-year-old face and he reached into a pocket in a coat on his chair and handed me a bill. Twenty dollars. Not bad.

I walked outside. I pulled out my new smokes and dug around for the matches. I took in a huge drag, and held it to my mouth before taking a long, deep breath in and out. The sweet, slightly hazy feeling in my head took the edge off. I hated this time of night, no matter where I was. The drunk guys on the streets were always scary. I felt the knife in my pocket rubbing against my thigh. I reached into the other one and felt the twenty dollars. I headed down 56th Street, under the viaduct and made a right at the light. Surely my mom would be passed out by now.

King Neptune Sucks off the World's Largest Potato!

Nikki Guerlain

Per our usual routine, we were watching strange-tittied women bend themselves to Tom Waits tunes at The Neon Boneyard.

My friend was soul sick and heart shattered, having received a Dear John letter from his would-be lover, The Gare Bear. Big, fat tears rolled down my friend's cheeks as he clenched the Dear John letter in his fat, meaty fist. "It's just like *When Harry Met Sally* but with more dick," he blubbered. "It's so sad."

It did not matter that my friend had not consummated his relationship with The Gare Bear, or that my friend was straight. What mattered was that this Gare Bear fellow had hurt my friend's feelings, and for that I had a good mind to go wherever he was and give him a piece of my mind.

Or, at the very least, apologize.

I went to snatch the tear-soaked letter from my friend's trembling paw but he resisted, sticking it between his legs, beyond my reach. He shook his head and snuffled pathetically as he continued to let his raw pussy emotions drip down his face. "Let's just put on our meat suits and set sail for rock bottom."

I'd had enough. I whipped out my mace and gestured in a threatening manner, demanding he give up the goods. "Give me the letter. Give it to me. I'm not joking. I'll do it! Give it up."

He was used to my mace threats but he handed me the letter anyways, making sure to look overly hurt at the idea that I'd spray him.

"For fucks' sake, man. Get a grip. There is no way it's as bad as you think it is. I mean, how could it even be a Dear John letter? You weren't even going out. You barely knew him."

He replied, "I wouldn't expect a person of your orientation to understand. We shared a moment. We locked eyes. It was magic. I could've done him, man. I could've done him. I've never felt that way before."

Personally, I'd never met the man. Hell, I didn't even know if he was a man. After all, it's not like my friend had never fallen in love with an inanimate object and he was overly fond of vegetables.

A server arrived to take our drink order. She had a middle-aged, ant-like face and wore a halter top that shoved her large dew sacks to just under her chin. She looked me straight in the eye and said, "You fuck like a girl."

My friend quit rocking and slapped the table, laughing. "That's right!"

Taken aback, I asked, "Excuse me?"

She said, "The drink special of the day. You Fuck Like a Girl."

"Well, in that case, we'll have two of those," I said.

She trotted off, her ta-tas boinky-boinking all the way to the bar.

My friend's lips curled into a ghoulish smile above his tear-swelled goo-goo eyes. "It's a sign, man. Can you feel it?"

But the only thing I felt was thirsty and impatient.

Ruffling through the multiple pages of the Dear John letter, I quickly realized that it was not, in fact, a Dear John letter but an invitation addressed to some guy named Goober for a party taking place at a bar called Hitler's Bunker.

I shoved it in front of my friend's face and waved it. "What is this? What is this?!"

My friend refused to make eye contact but instead spaced off while he blew big, wet raspberries at the server. She dropped off our drinks, ignoring my friend, and collected her money.

The raspberries stopped, replaced by a low rumbling in the distance. My friend drummed his fingers across the table. "You hear that? A storm is coming. How about we suck down these puppies then hit this party?"

I thought about chastising him for all the hullabaloo but he was my best friend, and we all, at one time or another, get upset over things that don't really exist, so I extended him the necessary empathy to let his little bitch fit over The Gare Bear go. Besides, when confronted with the fact that something you are emotionally invested in doesn't actually exist, the best course of action is to hop right on another path - one as fucked up as possible.

Given that the top of the party invitation was emblazoned with "King Neptune Sucks Off the World's Largest Potato!" this train wreck was as good as any. Although I was still a little irritated with my friend, I put on my best gung-ho face and readied myself to go, slamming my You Fuck Like a Girl in one fell swoop.

I said, "But first, we must go back to my place and pick up our roller skates and perhaps some music to listen to along the way."

By the time we had arrived back at the house and laced up our roller skates, I'd read through the invitation. Contained within were explicit instructions on how to get to Hitler's Bunker.

Hitler's Bunker was a bar and discotheque located on top of The Big Rock Candy Mountain in the third ring of hell, or so the invitation said. To get there, we would first need to locate some unicorns. In exchange for some artichokes, the unicorns would take us to a peg-legged pirate named Pig, a sort of gatekeeper to hell. We were to give him this invitation which would allow us passage below.

At first glance, the main problem would be in locating the artichokes as they were out of season. The unicorns, my friend assured me, would be taken care of as soon as we found the artichokes.

"Wherever there are artichokes, there are unicorns. Don't you know anything, man?" he said, shaking his head in admonishment for my apparent stupidity regarding uni behavior.

Still a little miffed at my friend's earlier manipulations for pity, I almost launched into a defensive tirade. I knew a lot about unicorns! But the prospect of watching a titan slick rick a giant tuber steered me back around to the tasks at hand and I let his little insult go. Back on track, I intuited that in order to find artichokes, we would need tunes and not just any tunes.

One would expect that when on roller skates in search for artichokes, one would require the musical mojo of Olivia Newton John or ELO, but that kind of stuff was for your average silly gooses. And we were not your average silly gooses. We were intrepid explorers of realms unknown. Psychonauts of the fly agaric persuasion. Good guys, basically. And great roller skaters.

It wasn't long until we'd scrolled our iPods appropriately to Juice Newton, adjusting our Bose headphones to high.

For a while, we skated in circles, but then *Angel of the Morning* took hold and we found ourselves in the middle of the produce section of Trader Joe's. Sure enough, in front of a display of artichokes were two queer-looking fellas with small wings and toilet paper tubes taped to their foreheads.

They were in mid-argument.

The big, black unicorn threw back his full mane of hair and jabbered, "Boy, her vagina is as deep as the Marianis Trench - her heart, as cold as the Antarctic."

The small, white one whinnied back, "What? Did you think that after the good 'doctor's' shaky hands botched her abortion that she was going to go to some coat hanger factory in the sky?! You kidding, dawg! Of course she ended up on your doorstep. You ain't that lucky." Then he stamped and snickered.

"So I said, no way, byatch! No way that bay-bay come from this pizzle. Cuz I came in yo butt. Now, I know you remember that. Cuz you said like, you couldn't trot straight for a week."

"You tell 'em, Bob."

"Oh, I did, Randy. I did."

My friend's left eye began to twitch. Clear evidence that he was on the brink of being sucked into some domestic drama that would again send him spiraling over The Gare Bear.

I had to take the reins on this one. I cleared my throat to get their attention. "Excuse me. Excuse me?" I said. "We're in the market for your services."

Big Black Bob backed up, raising his eyebrow up to his taped-on, toilet paper tube horn.

"Oh, you are, huh? Gonna let Big Black Bob come in yo big butt just so you can come back later and demand monies from me for the bay-bay you didn't have sucked out of yo butt?! No thank you. Been there, done that. Nuh-uh."

"You tell 'em, Bob!"

"Thanks, Randy."

The unicorns turned their backs to us and began discussing the weather. This seemed to unnerve my friend enough to break him out of his reverie. He jumped up and pumped his fist, yelling at them in guttural chunks of verbiage, "We've got a right! To go to this party! And you're going to take us!" Then he lunged over the uni's and grabbed two artichokes and deftly stuffed them into their mouths.

He screamed for me to jump on. Seeing that Bob was the closest, I jumped onto his back while my friend mounted Randy. Then we were off, our skate wheels spinning midair, headed to Pig the Pirate - Gatekeeper of Hell.

Until then, I had never understood the association between unicorns and rainbows. I'd always assumed it was some mystical fetish in the same line as fat girls and glitter. But, right then, on Bob's big, glossy back, I understood. I understood as we traversed space, time and even Earth, immersed in the sparkly glow of ROY G. BIV.

But the ride was almost over as soon as it started. And although we had dove deep into the earth, to the fiery belly of Hell, we remained squeaky clean and remarkably cool.

As soon as we slipped off our respective unicorns, they began to trot away.

"Wait! I cried after them. "But, how will we get back?!"

The uni's chimed back in unison, "Why, you take the elevator back, of course!" Then they were gone in a scattering of prism light.

My friend was visibly cheered. He said, "First, we find this peg-legged Pig man, then we secure some tacos!"

I could tell from the large smile on my friend's face, and the glee in his voice, that my friend was breaking out of his downward spiral and would soon forget about all this business with The Gare Bear. So far, this trip had all the appearances of being just fucked enough to swing him back on course, to prevent him from breaking down again over his imaginary, unrequited quest with that man, if he was even a man at all.

We weren't skating long before we heard a cheery *A Yo-Ho-Ho and a Bottle of Rum* floating across the Mars-like landscape. A funny, round figure toddling underneath an enormous tree came into view and the singing became louder. The figure ran into the tree trunk and fell down only to pick himself back up and immediately do it again. We approached him carefully, our invitation in hand. He ambled over to meet us when we were merely a few feet from the trunk of his enormous tree.

"Ahoy! Aren't ye a sight fer sore eyes. I ask ye, do ye come fer me booty? Or did ye come fer me t' be in yer booty?" He snickered. "Wha's th' secret password now 'n I shall allow ye in passage… "

I knew not of any secret passwords. I fumbled as I handed him the invitation, my hand accidentally smacking his peg leg. It was rough and splintery and covered in goo. I caught myself before visibly recoiling, fearful of his response.

He flipped through the papers, and seeing that everything was in order, replied cheerfully, "Oh, I see aye. Ye be wantin' fun passes. O' course! Ye ain't dead. Dunno how I could've missed that! Ye can nah be boardin' Davy Jones' locker if yer nah dead, unless ye be havin' fun passes."

"Yes, yes. We need to go to the party there." I pointed to the bar on the invitation.

"Okay, okay. Well, I'll let ye pass. But if ye be wantin' t' go down thar then ye'll needs t' pay Charon."

An elevator door formed in the trunk of the tree. The doors opened to display a lone, dark and gaunt figure in an oversized emerald-green hoodie, his hand operating a crank attached to a cage made of sticks and bones. Charon waved his skeletal hand at us. His voice was remarkably gay and feathery and lispy for being of such bad-ass fame. He spoke to Pig, "Oh, hi Larry. Stho happy to sthee you. What we got here?"

"Oh, naught much. Ust a couple o' lads wantin' t' party at Hitler's Bunker."

The pirate swigged rum then pulled coins out of his pocket. I went to grab the coins for our passage, but he snatched the coins away.

"Nah so fast, lads. Wha' are ye goin' t' do fer me? Me peg be partial t' anus."

Then he stamped his gooey leg into the red dirt of the ground and laughed from his belly.

I could tell my friend was just as puckered as I was, although he had not quit smiling.

Charon shook his hoodied head at the pirate, "Larry, the lasth thing that peg needs isth more assth. Now, you sthtop it."

"I be jus' kiddin'. Ye'll be gettin' enough o' that at Hitler's Bunker. Here ye go." Then he flipped a coin into each of our hands.

With more than a little trepidation, we rolled over to the figure in the stick-and-bone cage and handed him our coins. His hand was bone-wrapped in ivory leather and his breath was as cold as ice, even if his words were warm and friendly. He said, "That guy, he cracksth me up! Stho you boysth headin' out to Hitlersth Bunker to sthee the big water dude sthuck potato pole? I heard itsth going to be off the nut."

As he shut the door, I caught my friend trying to peek under Charon's knee-length hoodie. I pinched my friend's butt to get his attention, not wanting to start any trouble with the dead dude who, presumably, would take us back home after we were through partying.

As we descended through the layers of hell, I cleared my throat to catch Charon's attention. "So, will we need anything to get back home after we're done?"

Charon handed us parking validation tickets. "Justh get the guysth at the bar to punch the ticketsth for you and I'll take you back, okay?"

The elevator came to a halt and the door opened to a bum's delight— this had to be The Big Rock Candy Mountain. "Well, here you go! Justth follow the river up. Have fun, guysth and I'll sthee you later! Be sthafe!"

My friend said, "You know, that Charon guy was really nice. Hell isn't like anything I'd imagined."

"Yeah," I said. "There's certainly a lot more water than I thought there'd be."

"And lemonade and gin too!" my friend said, excitedly. Then he skated over to a fountain of lemonade overflowing into a gin spring and dropped to his knees and drank his fill. After he was done, he punched his fist out and grabbed a chicken tottering by. He got to his feet and lifted the chicken over his head and squeezed a hardboiled egg out of the hen straight into his mouth, then dropped the chicken on his way back to me.

I reached over and snagged two lit cigarettes from a tree and handed him one. "You certainly can't shake a stick at that."

I smiled. Fearful that we'd never get to The Bunker, I decided not to partake of the gin spring but lapped at the lemonade fountain before proceeding to dig my skates up the hill with my friend. The Bunker was within sight when I turned to my friend and said, "I don't think that was normal lemonade. I feel kind of funny." My friend replied, but it was all subharmonic bass warbling.

A sort of slug-textured red man let us into the door and showed us to some seats made of blue flame. My friend unbuckled his pants and joined some extremely large, knobby potato on stage. Something with a leathery-green hand put a flaming eggnog in front of me and I gulped it down greedily as if I was very cold, although I knew that I should've been very warm.

My mouth opened in a silent scream as my friend inserted a fist-sized potato protuberance into his butt and trumpets went off. Entering stage left, King Neptune came riding a sparkly wave of flame along with an octopus, two dolphins, a sea turtle, a lobster and twelve fish.

Wow.

He approached my potato-impaled friend and said, "I came all the way from Atlantis for this, my friend. For us to share this potato in connubial bliss. So, I ask you, will you be my hairy-chested bride?"

My friend perked up, as he choked out some kind of yes, and the raw pussy emotions once again flowed down his face. But not due to The Gare Bear.

Success.

The flaming eggnogs or the tainted Big Rock Candy lemonade must've been getting to me. I uncontrollably fist-pumped the air as King Neptune took a large potato protuberance into his mouth and noisily sucked it off as my friend simultaneously worked the other end.

I gulped down another flaming nog and *Gangsta's Paradise* began to play in the background. *Beat that, Gare Bear!* I thought. This is just what the doctor ordered.

The boys were still going at the potato, when to my surprise, Charon joined me at my table. He said, "There'sth no way in hell I wasth going to missth thisth. And I knew you guysth could hang, stho I sthought I'd drop by. I hope you don't mind."

He'd put on a pair of pink rhinestone-studded glasses on the void of his face, and though I could not see his lips, I knew he was smiling. "Oh, I sthee you like my glasses. They are pretty cool and it'sth stho bright down here, esthpecially after you've had a few hitsth of thisth." Then he handed me a smoking roach and we pounded knucks.

It could've taken hours or merely minutes for the whole debacle to play out. I don't know. What I do know is that I made a new friend that night, and that the fries tasted suspiciously of fish and ass— which, in some odd way, reminded me of The Gare Bear.

Could it be …? Ah, but who cares?

Fuck The Gare Bear and his nonexistent Dear John letter. This was our hot potato and we were going to fist pump it, and otherwise, to the "That's right!" "Stho coo!" "Right arm!" bloody end.

Russian Doll

Baz Nova

He finished wiping his plain, black-rimmed glasses with the white, sleeveless t-shirt he was wearing, then slumped down in front of his laptop. It was 3:27 a.m., according to the small time display in the bottom right-hand corner of the rectangular screen. He assumed it was accurate, seeing as he was under the impression that times and dates were usually set by the internet itself. Although he was never one-hundred-percent certain if this was a fully correct assumption, as his mobile phone often showed it to be around one minute before the time stated on his computer's screen. This perplexed him greatly, given that as far as he was aware, there was only one internet. Not some deranged, omnipresent multi-verse type affair; in which an infinite different internets all exist at the same place in space and time simultaneously, as if they were all being piled in together like on a rush-hour Japanese train. A question quickly arose in his head as to what would happen if one of those internets over there bumped into one of these other internets over here? Would it cause a total reverse polarity of the space-time continuum that would force every soulless, pop-peddling, cunt scab to disappear off of the face of the earth? To be chased back up into the unholy and barren wombs which spawned each and every one of their hollow, black hearts by the ugly noise they themselves created. But, being heard through people-with-tastes' ears? He hoped so.

He then decided that it was perhaps a distraction contemplating such trivial matters and, that these type of musings were better left for another time. Besides, he had another beast to tame.

He booted the program up that he used for scribbling with keys and stared at the blank, white screen - an image he was growing worryingly accustomed to. Now, it's not that he wasn't having any ideas to write, far from it to be honest, in fact, pretty much daily he would have several thousand new possibilities of creativity enter his cloudy sphere of thought. As if tiny half-dreams decided to sail the stormy, rough seas into his mind on little paper boats; lightning bolts of creativity scorching awesome into the sides of every vessel. Just the problem was, knowing which ones were golden and which chewed rotting goat's anus by the toothless mouthful. A conundrum that all creative types came up against at some time in their lives. Well, that's what he thought at least, and figured he was most likely right, too.

Quietly, he sat for an unknown amount of time with the blank screen staring straight back at him, his fingers hovering over the keyboard's keys, eagerly waiting to spring into action, hoping that the little boats of solid content would float on by, assembling dutifully into his squinted eyes' view, then one of the miniature, paper dream-boat captains would shout out gruffly above the wind and rain, "Oi, fuckface! We got's a good'un 'ere. Come grabs us up and dock's this shit into your brain box!"

But they didn't come, nothing did. Just an ugly, blank screen and a desolate blank mind, a travesty, to be true. Not one single iota of any idea he'd already had, and that was ready and waiting to be doused in ink, could be used for the job he had in hand currently. At least he didn't think so anyway. But persevere he must, being that the deadline was running dangerously short and his reputation depended on this piece. This was his foot in the door.

Picking up his cigarettes, he took one out, leaving seven still in the pack, and lit it up with a match. Inhaling deeply on the first pull, before exhaling all of the noxious, highly toxic fumes from his lungs. Like the rattly, half-hanging off exhaust pipe of an old, rusty three-wheeler van, early on a cold November morning, smoke bellowed outward from his slightly opened mouth and hit the empty screen that was taunting him in the gloomy darkness. He then took the cigarette from his mouth, flicked the tiny amount of ash that had gathered on the tip into the beer can/ashtray, then placed it back between his dry lips. His eyes still fixed continuously on the unchanging, white, empty mass in front of him. All he needed was the 'right' idea, and, for that to then be of a standard worth paying for. It was a different scenario than he was used to, getting paid work, and he really didn't want to fuck it up. But, as per usual, like his page, his mind remained blank.

Deciding that he needed a break from all this strenuous work he was doing, he vacated to the toilet, which can be said to be the only true safe haven for any artistic type. The cold, porcelain pot was going to be like ice against his bare ass cheeks, he knew that, and as he lowered himself down into the position, he braced himself for the inevitable impact. With gritted teeth, he sheepishly landed on the loo-nar surface, and with the careful precision of any average, half-drunken, semi-literate writer could do in the early hours of a cold winter's morning. The actual event itself passed without incident, other than when the toilet paper ran out halfway through the clean-up operation. Once finished, while washing his hands, he caught the sleepy reflection of himself in the bathroom mirror. He paused for a moment, stuck in his own gaze, not in a vain manner, nor in a self-pitying way, but with a questioning eye. Why couldn't he find the story he needed to write? Why was it being so elusive? Why the fuck was he still awake?

The realisation that he wasn't going to find an answer in the reflection of a tired man's eyes came soon enough. He shook off the echoes of his introspective pondering like raindrops on a wax jacket, freshly waterproofed and fearful of the damp. He left the toilet and walked back into his office space then sat back down in his chair, all the while still wondering if a plan of action would come kicking and screaming to his fingertips the instant he sat in front of the keyboard. Though no such joy would grace our protagonist as yet, and of course it may still never come at all.

INSPIRATION!

This is what he was seeking, but unfortunately, he hadn't actually been looking. Therefore, he was never really going to be able to find that which he sought. So, he decided to take steps in solving this puzzle, hoping dearly it would bear some delicious fruits for the labours he would so selflessly undertake. He would sleep, a deep and solid slumber, wishing that the images and words that were to be created from his twisting, painted, unconscious mind, would form an ugly monster to go and ravage the lands upon his will.

The bed was cold and unforgiving against his flesh, the feeling like frost on long grass clung to the sheets. Adjusting the covers so they folded under his feet, he glanced at the rising damp and black mold that was growing bigger and spreading like a drywall cancer as the winter days rolled onwards, until the milder days of spring. Being poor was a lifestyle he was accustomed to. If it wasn't broke, he didn't like it, Comfort was found in the damaged and un-useful; the wall suited him well.

His eyes shut. His body wanted to rest. His mind wouldn't shut the fuck up.

Lying, eyes closed, flat on his back, he tried to shut the busy train station in his skull off; silence the million options trying to keep him awake. Eventually, though he didn't know when, he drifted off.

NOTHING… thick, black, silent nothingness…

The alarm screamed out from his mobile phone at 11:30 a.m., buzzing and annoying. It was promptly put on silent with several expletives; he then slept for a further hour and a half. Waking up sometime around one in the afternoon, only to go to the bathroom for his daily cleansing ritual. Most of his countrymen had gotten up, gone to work and were now preparing for, or just finishing their lunches. While he was taking a shit and having a bath, not at the same time, I might add. Well, possibly once or twice as a child, maybe. Often, he thought about them as he went about his day. Albeit a day six hours behind the rest of his community and usually not filled with what most would class as traditional work.

For example, most would say looking online is just that, looking online, general browsing if you like. But, our intrepid wordsmith would say it was research. In fact, everything he did could fall under 'research.' An overheard drunken conversation in a bar between two of the local inbred bar-flies, having a shitty-minded, food-server's premenstrual attitude laid upon him when they gave the wrong order and he dared to voice an opinion of disappointment. It could be a split-second flash of inspiration when walking to the shops, or even a difficult wank. All of these and a million more could all be classed as research. He did a lot of research… not much writing, though.

After getting out from the bath and drying, he dressed, lit a smoke up, leaving six, then considered how best to spend his day. He knew the piece of writing was due, but he still couldn't find the right thing to write. So, he would look for the inspiration if it wouldn't come to him willingly.

He checked the time - 14:27 p.m. He checked the weather. Cold but dry. He decided that a walk would clear his mind and make way for a story. Collecting the things he would take with him - wallet, phone, cigarettes, keys, he left his room and went down the stairs to the front door. Opening, then locking it behind himself.

Outside was bitterly cold. Frost ran across the long blades of grass and dead leaves twitched in the slight but cutting breeze. He left the garden by a green gate, which had paint flaking off, turned left, then headed towards the lake near his home.

Seeing no one as he walked, the block he lived on seemed quieter than usual, but then it was only around three in the afternoon and freezing cold out, so it was understandable that the alleyways leading to the lake weren't bustling like Times Square on a new year's eve. Plodding along, he eventually came to the thin stretch of woodland that encircled the lake. Looking upwards to the trees, his eyes darted from branch to branch, trying to spot some kind of wildlife, be it bird or squirrel, or whatever for that matter. Anything to take his mind off not knowing what to write. He liked nature. He liked how simple it seemed. Basic needs. The common squirrel doesn't give a fiery, flaming fuck about reality television or soap operas. He could at least say he held that in common with the common squirrel of Britain, and he'd say it in a 'common' accent too. Common for Kent, at any rate.

The cold weather had brought rain with it as well as the frost. Large, semi-frozen puddles blocked his path in several places on the first corner of the lake. Several times he had to take his chances on the grass, where the possibilities of hidden puddles were very real. At one point, he even had to hop up onto a bench then leap off the other side. A distance of about four to five feet until the dry landing zone. A small, separate lake had formed across the entire path and also the grass opposite the bank. Though the bank itself wasn't submerged, it would have been an even tougher job trying to reach there and pass the mini-sea that way. Once this area was passed, he knew the rest of his wander would remain dry mostly. He often walked around the lake and had done so since his childhood.

Coming up on to a set of rocks that were used as a kind of art for the public, he saw a man and his son talking by the edge of the water. He stopped to smoke a cigarette and listened in on their conversation. He sat on a nearby bench and observed.

"Dad, why can't I play football like the others at school?" asked the boy, aged around six.

"What do you mean, mate?" replied his father, a burly man of around thirty-five.

"Well, they're all better than me at playing. Why?"

"Because some people are better at some things than others. That might just mean football isn't your thing. Don't worry yourself about it. When you grow up, you'll see there's more to life than just being able to kick a ball. You could be really good at science and become an astronaut, or if you really want to be good at football, just practice a lot. Practice makes perfect!" The man put an arm around his kid's shoulder reassuringly, then said:

"All you got to do is be yourself; happiness will follow."

The two then finished feeding the ducks and walked away.

The words bounced around inside his head.

The man was right. Beings one's self is the key to happiness, the key to everything, but more importantly, the key to his story.

Almost running home, he dashed straight through the puddles and back along the route he'd taken. Rushing into his home and directly up the stairs to his desk. Turning the computer on, he mulled over the recent events in his head. The advice stolen from a stranger.

Collecting all of the fragmented moments together, he sat down and lit another cigarette.

Now, leaving only four in the pack.

The program booted up and he took a deep drag.

Could this work? He didn't know, but he would still try.

He then poured the first of the day's drinks and focused hard on the blank screen. His fingers floated above the keys, he heard the captain's shouts above the fuzz to pull anchor, then started writing…

He wrote…

"He finished wiping his plain, black-rimmed glasses with the white, sleeveless t-shirt he was wearing, then slumped down in front of his laptop. It was 3:27 a.m…"

The Street Artist

Jeremy Maddux

The first time I saw Datura's street art, it happened like a snake bite: fast, precise, stealthy. I was loading groceries into the trunk. As I was heaving a watermelon out of the cart, my eyes caught an abstraction on the ground, something that wasn't supposed to be there. It was a chalk, cartoon rendering of a peacock with a smiling face on its endlessly colorful feathers. The peacock was pushing a cart of its own, much smaller. I didn't actually realize the intricacy of it until I shelved the buggy with the others. In this context, the peacock's hunched-over posture and annoyed face made total sense. It was as if I was parking my cart on top of the one it was loading. I wondered, who could have taken the time to do this? Who had such an eye for detail? I photographed it for posterity and sent it to friends back home through the social network of their choice. I thought it was the last time I would see the child-like chalk art; one of those rare moments that give you pause to reflect on the surprises our days can still offer.

When I got home, I checked my answering machine. Three hang ups and a call from my brother informing me that Mom fell again. It made me angry when she fell. I interpreted it as her giving up, or just not watching where she was going. I boiled spaghetti noodles with portabella mushrooms and black olives, then covered it with shavings of parmesan cheese until there was a sheet of it over the noodles and sauce. I had fixed more than I could eat, as usual. Not one for eating leftovers, I decided to dump it into the alley my apartment overlooked.

As I chucked the pot of cold spaghetti out over the cracked cement below, I froze to take in the sight of a three-dimensional spider's web, illustrated with such delicate precision that I temporarily believed there was a monstrous arachnid nesting down there. There were cans with wavy white lines painted over so that they appeared to be contents of the web. I went downstairs to get a better look. Part of the web had been designed across the dumpster. Had someone moved the dumpster even two inches off, the web would have lost its three dimensional effect. Then, I noticed chalk writing in the top-left corner of the web. It said, 'Datura, 2013,' illustrated and signed in chalk resembling the webbing. So my mysterious artist had a name. Datura. I loved the way it rolled around my mind and off my tongue.

Certain I'd heard the word somewhere before, I researched it. Datura was a flower relied on in India as a poison. It contained three different toxins: atropine, scopolamine and hyoscamine - all potent, all deadly. Also, for the few adventurous enough to cultivate it, it was used as a hallucinogen, although the physical side effects of ingestion always canceled out any benefits under the influence of datura.

It was three weeks before my third sighting. Being a single woman in the city increases the likelihood of boredom by thirty percent. I read those statistics somewhere. I did what any repressed city girl would do: I went to the bar, hoping to pick up someone or get picked up. I ordered a Blue Moon with an orange rind and sipped at it with dainty disinterest. I was waiting for the buzz so I could zone out, staring at the top shelf liquor I couldn't afford. Out of my peripheral vision, I saw something at the other side of the countertop. I moved to another bar stool to examine it. It was one of those charming, chalk art scribblings, courtesy of Datura. It was the peacock once again, who was lifting a long-necked beer bottle up to the lips of the smiley face on its mélange of colored feathers. The face was taking a gulp from the bottle. I waved down the bartender.

"Excuse me, sir? Do you know who drew this?"

With a towel over one shoulder, he wobbled toward me. I could tell by the scar on the back of his neck that he'd had major back surgery at some point. When he made it over, he leaned forward to examine it.

"Looks like a Picasso. How the hell should I know?" He removed the towel from his shoulder and went about wiping it clean. I stopped his hand with mine.

"Wait! What do you think you're doing?"

"Lady, I'm wiping this shit off the bar. This isn't an art gallery. If you don't release my hand in the next three seconds, you're out of my bar."

"If you wash off that drawing, you're out of your bar."

Next thing I knew, the bouncer was coming to collect me with a firm arm around my elbow. It was like a vice grip. I couldn't help but feel a little turned on, even if his physique did nothing to impress me. Well, I went there hoping somebody would take me out. I just didn't realize it would be to the sidewalk.

The only thing that bothered me was that I didn't get a chance to photograph Datura's newest piece. When I reached my car, I started to rummage through my things for the keys when I realized I had no things. I'd left my purse inside.

I edged back to the entrance to talk to the bouncer who'd bounced me before. I twirled a lock of hair around my finger, turning up the charm.

"Hi, you probably remember me from a few minutes ago. I understand your position, but I seem to have left my purse inside."

"Ma'am, the bartender does not want you back in here."

"I understand that, but my purse is in there. It has my keys, my money, everything! Can you get it for me?"

"My job is to patrol the door."

"Well, what about one of your buddies then?"

"It's just me."

"Maybe I'm not making myself clear here, or maybe the wheatgrass shakes are clogging up your brain. I. Can't. Leave. Without. My. Purse!"

"Looking for this?" asked a young man of about twenty-four to my right. The bouncer was staring holes through me, arms crossed beneath a face of incredulity. I almost wanted to take him for a test ride, but this kid fetched my purse for me. He would do. I snatched my purse from him, my eyes never leaving the bouncer.

"Thank you! It's good to see there are still some gentlemen left in this city!"

The bouncer rolled his eyes. "Ah, give me a break!"

With the acrid taste of defeat in my mouth, I fled the scene with the fetcher boy gaining traction. "Excuse me, miss? I saved the day. Can I at least bask in your glow before you exit my life forever?"

He had my attention. Depending on what came out of his mouth next, I was even considering taking him home with me. Hey, I don't mind rooting for the underdog from time to time.

"The reward comes in the deed itself, don't you think?" I asked, turning on my heel, taking in his wiry body, trying to see how we might sync up in an embrace.

"Absolutely, I would like to do many more good deeds for you! Thing is, my friend ditched me for some lush back at the bar. I have no ride."

"Well, one good turn deserves another. Hop in and we'll get you home, Sir Galahad."

As I turned the key in the ignition, I had a phallic flash, naughty thoughts of my passenger taking control, driving into me. He looked cute enough, but those hands of his were softer than mine. As he leaned right to buckle himself in, I had another Freudian impulse; keys and locks, belts and buckles everywhere, the entire city laid bare for me as one giant mechanism of lever and fulcrum, man and woman. When he settled back, I saw the outline of his chest through his shirt. He actually had muscles, thank God! Periodically, I stole glances panning ever downward. Then, I saw what he was packing as it lay across the top of his thigh.

"So, what's your name?" I asked.

"Brendan."

"Where do you live, Brendan?" If he told me, it didn't register. Datura's art had stirred up quite a storm within me.

"Uh, you were supposed to take a right back there."

"We're taking a little detour. Hope you don't mind."

"Not at all. Detour to where?"

I flashed him the hellcat glance to let him know where he stood with me. This new generation of man-boys seriously lacked subtlety.

"Fine by me," he said, so excited now that I felt a little embarrassed for him. He marveled at my ability to parallel park without incident. As I fumbled for the apartment key, I noticed a parking meter across the street. It was yet another example of Datura's handiwork. This time, it was a cartoon rendition of Mayor Bloomberg, framed high up on the brick wall, in such a way that it appeared he was sitting on the parking meter. To be more succinct, it appeared that the Mayor had a pole up his ass, which he did. Of course, you could only see this from my vantage point across the street. Pedestrians on the other side of the street would simply see Bloomberg falling in freeform with a look of astonishment on his face. It was like it was designed specifically to capture my attention, like a dedication from a secret admirer. But that had to be wishful thinking. I had the young, virile boy in my custody, and would have to make do with him. For now.

133

"Wow, they really outdid themselves this time, huh?"

"Do you know who leaves these?"

"I have a pretty good idea. But he doesn't like to be bothered, so he leaves the name 'Datura' on all of his work."

"Who is he?"

"I'll explain later. It's a long story."

I hoped his story would prove longer than the intercourse. My knight in shining armor lasted exactly four minutes and fifty three seconds, and two of those were spent undressing. It was a great shame he hadn't learned to properly apply the monster at his disposal. With a little more practice, he could use it to tame even the most fiercely independent woman. He was like a cub scout with a gatling gun. I didn't want to let on how much his 'prematurity' vexed me, so I patted him on the head and laughed, then got up to wash his seed out of me. I don't know what I would have done if he had impregnated me.

After washing up, I found him slightly sulking in the dining room over a cigarette. Whatever he was smoking, it was clearly an inferior brand. Even our tastes in cigarettes clashed. In nothing but my bathrobe, I pulled up a seat beside him. Sitting at the other end of the table would send the wrong signal, plus the cold shoulder isn't something I have much use for in my arsenal. He'd obviously not been with a woman in a long time, so I gave him the benefit of the doubt.

"So, you said you knew Datura personally?"

"Some days I do," he said with a smirk, putting out his cigarette in my ashtray with the wood carving of a deer at the bottom. "What would you like to know?"

"Who is he? Was he self-taught or did he go to art school? Is he religious? Married or divorced? How does he take his coffee?"

"I was self-taught, never spent a day in university. I'm a secular Catholic, never married. I take my coffee with a tablespoon of whipping cream."

It took me a minute to process what he was saying. A curtain of silence hung between us. "You're the artist?"

He looked uncomfortable, like he regretted saying anything. "Guilty as charged. No one else knows. I'd like to keep it that way."

"Oh my God! There's so much I want to say!" This was true. What I wanted to say most of all was that the gift was wasted on a weakling like him. I was disappointed, going through the motions, saying everything I envisioned myself saying to Datura in the event I ever met him. "Every time I see your work in public, it reminds me I'm alive! How do you bring it into three dimensions? I can't believe you've had no formal training!"

"I was always a whiz at geometry, stuff like that." A whiz. That's all he could give me for an answer. He was a whiz at geometry. The one thing that had brought me back to life in this shithole of a city was deflating before me. I wanted to throw myself under a pillow and curl up in a ball, but I had to find a creative way to kick him out first.

"So, that was you back at the bar? The drawing on the counter?"

"None other," he said, smiling, proud to confirm his identity. Maybe too proud.

"Before you leave, could you draw up an original piece for me?"

"I like my work to be spontaneous. It's why I don't do commission."

"Oh, come on, so the night won't be a total loss!" He cringed as I said this.

"Even if I wanted to, I don't have my supplies with me."

"What did you use on the counter back at the bar?"

"I used chalk, same as always," he said, swallowing.

"But you don't have it on you?"

"I must have left it at the bar."

"But you remembered my purse. How selfless!" I couldn't help it. This twerp was digging himself deeper with every word.

"I told you, my friend abandoned me to go home with a chick."

"A chick? Why, that scoundrel! So, tell me, O Champion of Virtue, how do you find the time to do your elaborate street art when you're not retrieving women's purses for them?"

"Maybe I should go."

"That's a million dollar idea, ace! Go with that instinct!"

With his face now beet-red, he grabbed a fistful of his leather jacket and scrambled for the door. I lit a cigarette of my own, from a far superior brand, then muttered, "Putz" to myself as I reflected on what I'd allowed this imposter, this poseur, to do to me. Spying his weak, effeminate brand of cigarettes on my table, I chased after him. It was exhilarating to know I was about to throw them at him!

"Don't forget your Menthols, metro boy!" I shouted, hurling them at him as he disappeared down Beach Street. He didn't even bother turning around to retrieve them. I looked where they fell, then staggered in place. They'd landed in the alley, but it was no alley I remembered seeing before. Strangest of all, there were no trashcans, dumpsters, cardboard boxes or hobos frequenting it. It felt as new as it seemed. I sauntered further through this new frontier of New York, the alley seeming to extend for miles in the distance. Lips of sky kissed the brick and mortar. It felt like I was inside Datura's street art, a lone figure exploring the enigmatic new corridor. I walked on for some time, but got no further. It took only a few steps to recede back to the entryway, where I found myself staring at Datura's construct of an alleyway under open sun, his name etched into the lush, bluish-gray of illustrated cement. I picked up the pack of cigarettes to test out my theory. When I tossed it at the chalk alley on the wall, it landed within its perimeters, like an extension of the street. I was dizzy with excitement. No one else seemed to notice anything askew. This was my own private exhilaration.

After that, my encounters with Datura ceased without warning. When I retraced my steps back to all the places he had decorated, they were scrubbed clean as if they had never existed. In one of my more irrational moments, I called a news reporter and tried to convince them I was the one leaving the mysterious art all around town, but they didn't even know what I was talking about.

There I was in one of the biggest cities in America and felt smaller than the insignificant life I'd fled in Illinois. I took an art class at the community college hoping to espy someone to stifle my boredom and ennui, but they only made it worse. None of them had heard of my artist friend either. I attended a poetry group hoping to quell my insensate longing, but they had words for things I didn't even know were things (Couplets, Iambic pentameter, Ekphrastic poetry), and would often shift abruptly to speaking in a foreign tongue as if they were insulting me so I couldn't hear them. Plus, the music at the coffee house sounded like a swarm of bees yodeling. I even tried church, but it felt like being in a museum where everyone's sadness was an exhibit. By the third Sunday, I gave up. I think they were glad I didn't return.

In light of all my failed experiments, I did what everyone did who had exhausted all other options. I turned to pharmaceuticals. Of course, my doctor started me out on the weak stuff (Citalopram, Cymbalta), but it didn't take much prodding on my part to get moved up to the honeymoon suite of medicines (Valium, Ativan). I could almost tolerate days in the city with the help of my new friends.

I was required to see a counselor regularly while taking these medications which was understandable. There, on a wall behind the secretary's desk, was that inimitable style of the stranger I knew so well: A fresco painting lush with aquavelva-blue, charcoal-gray and ivory-white. Best of all, the painting was of children gathered in a perfect circle, laughing, holding hands. No grudges or disputes, but eternally at play. I don't remember bypassing the secretary to get a close up, but I must have, because the next thing I knew, the secretary was pivoted in her seat to ask me why I was behind her desk. My hands were on the painting. My psychiatrist gave me a look of bewilderment as he called me into the office for our weekly session.

"Who did the painting in the lobby?" I asked.

"You know, I can't remember off the top of my head." He was so busy scribbling notes that he didn't see me roll my eyes at him. "I believe it started with a 'D,' though. It was one of those flamboyant names like Prince or Madonna."

"Would you be interested in selling it?"

After what felt like an hour of haggling, he agreed to my proposal, and I was one hundred and sixty dollars poorer, counting the cost of the session. We also talked about my soiree with the insouciant man-child. He interpreted my sudden interest in art as some personal breakthrough, but it was merely a silver lining in what I considered a very dark cloud.

I framed the painting that night to replace some battered print of a wolf in the snow. I stood back and marveled again at the immensity and unpretentiousness of it - lively children in the warm, tangerine sun. There were no political factions or personal differences, not even an agreement to disagree. It seemed like every exchange I had in my adult life required some sacrifice on my part: time, money, energy, affection. I was constantly having to mete out varying degrees of compromise. Truly, every scrap out here in the city of angels had to have some claimant. If it didn't, they just hadn't heard of it yet.

I paced through my apartment as I am prone to do when excited, studying my new acquisition from every vantage point: the kitchen, the bathroom, the living room where it was framed. It reminded me of a scene from my own youth, my eighth birthday party. Mom was still in good health then, positively vibrant. She'd taken me and several friends to the park. This was back when there were still a million things to do at the park. We played jump rope, used the swings and slides, played tag. Mom laid out a blanket and we ate lunch. Then, I opened my presents. My friends were all so happy to be with me. Then, Mom invented a new game where we had to run as far as we could while holding each other's hands. If we fell, we had to sit out the next round. It was around the fifth try that I remember becoming self-aware of the joyous time I was having, and how times should always be like this. It was the longest Saturday afternoon I'd ever enjoyed, and it felt like it would never end.

I snapped out of my reverie then, transported back to my mundane apartment setting, fresh tears brimming up over my eyelids. As I studied the painting, I recognized the face of every child holding hands (Sean Tiptree, Shelly Bergen, Teddy Montrose, Cassie Ellington, Sheila Caldwell, ME), and the grown woman on the stretched-out blanket in the background (my mother). I realized then that my recent experience wasn't new at all. I'd been living out Datura's brushstrokes and chalk doodles all along. It was the only sensible explanation. I broke down despite all the pills I'd consumed and heaved myself into the wall with all the force within me. I reached out to touch the painting, hoping to penetrate it and leave my murky existence behind. It granted no such purchase. I cried out, hoping the artist would hear me somehow.

"Why won't you let me in? All I ever wanted was for someone to know me. Why can't I know you?" I collapsed against the wall, swooning into a kind of submission. Sleep followed. I woke up the next morning with my alarm clock sounding off in the next room. After disarming the buzzing menace, I threw water on my face, noting all the redness and puffy rings from crying, as well as fresh, new tears chasing the old ones. A few Valiums and Phentermines later, I was good as new and scolding myself for being such a crybaby the night before.

As things wound down at work, I had an epiphany. If I couldn't meet the artist, I would become one myself. I picked up a brush, paints, a canvas and an easel from the store. As I carried them up the steps to my apartment, a middle-aged man, hunched over with the classic symptoms of osteoporosis, approached me to ask if I knew Jesus.

"No, do you?" I asked, before moving on. A week before, he'd been drifting up and down this street to ask for money. It felt strangely suitable that he was now talking down his horn-rimmed glasses at me, who actually bothered to give him money that day. I was all out of charity. I cleaned up the living room to make space for my new pet project. I stared for much of the afternoon at the blank canvas before me. My eyes periodically wondered to my purchase the previous night, the deceptive simplicity of it. With the amount of colors Datura implemented, I wasn't convinced it could be as easy as the final product appeared to be.

I focused in my mind on what the artist might look like. That was what I wanted to paint most of all. I imagined him with long, stringy black hair and crow's feet under his eyes, then promptly tore it up and threw it away. I tried picturing him as white, black, red and yellow; stoic, picaresque, romantic and jovial, but one thing that never changed in every attempt was the fact I was painting a man. I tore up my seventh attempt, starting fresh once again. The time was now on its way to 10:30 and I faced a work day full of what I'd eluded today. My brushstrokes were hard and clinical, like I was striking at every human being that had ever hurt or taken advantage of me. At precisely 1:27 a.m., I had finished painting my representation of the artist, a spry young woman with dark, rimmed glasses, a tattoo of a heart on her chest, peeking out of her cropped top, a smile of perspicacity, unpretentious eyes completely uninterested in the politics of sex. She felt more real to me than my own reflection.

I was convinced she was out there somewhere, one more lost soul in a city filled to capacity with lost souls. I endeavored to find her. I started my search at an alternative art forum online called Artistic Indulgence. I posted my collection of Datura-related photos and waited. These were the responses I got:

Kitty218: These look awfully familiar. Are you sure they're not public domain?

Bryan_Shaffer2012: They remind me of that art that's meant to go viral, like Banksy or Zinn.

Renaissance Jerk: No shit, Sherlock. These are obviously contributions to the street art movement. To the person who posted these, the style definitely rings a bell and I'm certain I've heard that artist's name before. It wasn't in New York, though. It was here in Atlanta, so you might start your search there.

I typed in every possible string of search terms (Datura + Art + Atlanta, for one) before I finally hit pay dirt. I turned up an article in the *Atlanta Journal-Constitution* that read, 'Teen claims vandalism was artistic statement.' Her name in the article was Samantha Hain. The teen pictured in the photo resembled a younger version of the woman in my painting. It was either a coincidence or kismet, and I don't believe in coincidences. I called the school and solicited them about Samantha Hain, but the principal was uncomfortable disclosing information about past students. He provided me with a number so I could continue my research.

It was Gladys Yarborough I reached out to. She was a former art director who was employed at the school at the time of the news article. To allay her suspicions, I convinced her I was there on a journalism assignment. I even brought a fake resume overflowing with blank pages. Thankfully, she didn't insist on examining it.

"You don't mind if I grade papers while we talk, do you?" I shook my head. "So why the sudden interest in Samantha?" she asked, marking several x's in a row. She mouthed the student's name in frustrated silence. It looked like she said, 'Noah'.

"I believe that she's the famous artist Datura who's been leaving graffiti all over Manhattan."

"Datura, eh?" she said, taking a dainty sip of coffee. "Haven't heard that name in years."

"Then it is her," I said. Miss Yarborough selected her next words with caution.

"Samantha's father considered himself an explorer of sorts. He wrote several books and essays on what he termed the 'invisible world.' He believed one could reach a higher plane of existence through psychoactive substances: mushrooms, peyote, mescaline, yage, *datura*... Real Terrence McKenna stuff. He was often on speaking tours, giving six hour seminars on opening the third eye. At first glance, he would seem like an eccentric character and nothing more. But Samantha suffered without a father at home. She was always drawing faraway places where she thought her father might be."

"The arrest. Tell me about the arrest."

"From what I understand, Samantha first discovered the idea from a commissioned street painting. You can still see it at the side of Jersey's Bar and Grill downtown. She decided she wanted to do something similar, so she took up graffiti. Spray painted this beautiful piece on the wall of a church back lot. It was this field of crosses, but if you looked close enough, the field was in the shape of a human hand. It was gripping the biggest cross at the center. The congregation didn't appreciate it, and so it became what it became."

"Where is her father now?"

"Well, that's the million-dollar question. No one knows. He vanished before she was out of high school."

"What do you mean 'vanished'?"

"It's a controversial topic that has no real explanation. He was giving a lecture about spiritual enlightenment. There was a screen with all these symbols, and... he disappeared into it." I was immediately reminded of my own submersion into Datura's faux alleyway.

"What was his name?"

"Edward Hain. You can still find some of his books in retailers, but most of them are out of print now."

I stopped off at the nearest library to see what I could find. If her father was as well-known as she claimed, they would have records of him, remembrances, maybe even original manuscripts of his work. All I found was an old article through microfiche. *Lecture Ends with Man's Disappearance*. A strange thing happened as I puzzled over the document. Everyone in the library stopped what they were doing and regarded me with a malicious stare. They were positively hostile as their eyes glowered in disgust. I felt threatened, even violated by their jagged stares. I got up to leave thinking they might even resort to violence. Then, a voice penetrated the silence.

"Excuse me, miss?" I turned to identify the voice. It was an older gentleman I'd been sharing a table with. He leered down the spectral barrels of his horn-rimmed glasses and extended his hand. At first, I thought it was to touch me or wring my neck. His actions seemed detached from and inconsistent with his mannerisms.

"You forgot this." He held my purse by one strap and gingerly returned it to me. I accepted it despite my reticence to be within arm's length of him. It was as if I had tripped some existential wire, or arrived too close to the naked truth, and now, the agents of these and other revelations were scrambling to cover up, to return me to a consensus reality. Either I'd come dangerously close to cracking some code or I was going crazy. At that point, I welcomed either possibility. I returned home with more questions than answers.

As I shuffled around the metropolitan circus that is New York, the atmosphere seemed to crackle with a new life. I walked with no intended direction for as long as I could, following paths and streets to their logical ends, transferring from one destination to the next. I realized that life was a sequence of destinations. There was no escape from this because every place existed as a form of spatial restitution. Darkness came first and light followed. Darkness retreated in defeat. Light's been corrupting ever since. My thoughts were becoming stranger all the time, unrecognizable. I walked until I found myself in the Bowery. I had made it pretty far without being mugged or raped, which was surprising. Then, I saw a new masterwork. It was the painting on the wall that broke my trance. I ignored the wino pissing on the wall and stepped over another to get to it. It was oddly shaped, like an incomplete work with gaps that needed filling. The principal perspective was of a night sky, with stars like tiny fireflies and someone's hand capturing a few of them in a bottle. The hand belonged to no one as the piece was incomplete. Still, I could see what Datura was going for, and it would have been beautiful had she completed it. I speculated that Datura was interrupted mid-brushstroke and had to leave in a hurry. I made a decision right then and there that I would stay there until she came back. I paid the meager fee to the innkeeper. Just like that, I was a guest at the run down Sunshine Hotel. As I moved through every ramshackle corridor, my presence roused all manner of fetid, impoverished animals. I was happy to get to my room. I started to rethink how much Datura's secrets really meant to me. What if she was murdered by some derelict? What if I suffered a similar fate? The thought was almost too much to bear, that such a brilliant mind and steady hands should be mortal at all.

When I heard a commotion outside my door, then realized that there was nothing separating me from the other rooms but a roof of chicken wire, I scooted the dresser drawer against the door to prevent any intrusions. This whole expedition was insane.

I was about to top my insanity with a midnight stroll through the absolute worst place for a midnight stroll. Rape Central. At this point, the only thing I feared was never knowing the central answer to the Datura mystery. I was driven by a compulsion I barely understood to chase this stranger through any conceivable distance of night. I would arrive at some measure of meaning before this was over. There was no hobo or hoodlum who would impede my pursuit. I put myself in Datura's shoes. If I were an artist, where would I go in the Bowery? It appeared that she'd given up on the star painting she'd started then abandoned. I checked in an abandoned warehouse, stepping across both biological and organic debris. A winsome bark of laughter cut through the night. I traced it to a church parking lot. I remembered the art teacher's story about how a young Samantha tried to improve the church just a tiny bit by adding some art to its foundations. Crossing the church property, it was the first time I felt warm that night. In the back lot, I saw my destiny. There on the wall was a swirling vortex, stationary, but pulsating with invitation. I knew by the way the bricks jiggled that someone had just moved through it. I was quick to follow. I reached out with my foot to find the purchase of the threshold. It was like stepping into a swimming pool, only static energy crackled against my skin. I followed after. There, at the center of the distortion was the woman I sought. She didn't seem surprised to see me.

"Well, how disappointed are you?" she asked, twirling a piece of twine around her finger with the manic abandon of a pixie girl.

"I'm still holding out hope for a religious experience."

"Religious experience," she repeated after me with a dramatic flourish.

"How does it all work?" I asked, marveling at the artwork we currently inhabited.

"It's not as earth shattering as you might think. For every strange door out there, you can bet there's a key somewhere. My dad had a lot of keys."

She started to move away from me. Although there were no visible exits, I could tell she was about to leave.

"Please, let me stay with you. There are no new things left in the world. I've searched so hard."

"There are no new things," she said. I couldn't tell if she was correcting or agreeing with me. She brushed my bangs behind my ear and pulled me in for a kiss on the forehead. It was quick but sincere, like a bee sting, but not as painful. If she'd completed this movement like we were lovers, her next action was to regard me as a long lost friend. She scooped me up in the most unpretentious embrace I'd felt since first grade.

"I will release you from your sadness," she promised in a voice that was almost cooing with empathy for my lost little life. She didn't offer me drugs or pull a gun. Instead, she issued a quizzical list of banal instructions which I was to follow to the letter.

So I made my exodus out of the vortex on the church wall, out of the Bowery and out of hopelessness. I retired to my apartment, locked the door and shuttered the living room shades until all external stimuli was blotted out. I lied down in my bedroom, which seemed just a little brighter now (even with the blackout drapes). I unfastened my left bra strap and let it hang off of me like a sling. I gazed up at the ceiling until it enraptured my full attention.

"Don't worry if you don't see anything at first," she had cautioned, "keep focusing until the picture starts to form. When it does, you'll know my latest work has begun."

I poured everything I had ever been into that piercing stare. I began to imagine pieces of ceiling rearranging, ricocheting and pirouetting just like the clouds did when I was a child. There was no death then. Now, it crops up everywhere, like a fungus, a malignant discoloration of all things vibrant and pristine. Datura has rescued me from the covetous abyss.

Now, I float forever, suspended in an instant, borne on dreamlike currents. It sounds like Purgatory or a trap, but I promise you, I am freer now than I was across the entirety of my life. I am exalted above and outside of time. Children and their elderly counterparts look upon me with simultaneity, opposing fixtures of mortality. When I gaze back at them, I am no longer afraid to say I'm alive. I will never fall down like my mother.

Contributor Biographies

Trevor Neal

Trevor Neale lives near the ocean in Portsmouth, England and is probably best known for making ladies swoon on Twitter - TheBogfather @mojonathan73.

He has been writing poetry for about six years and a large collection of his widely varied body of works can be found at http:/hebogfather.webs.com/

Why TheBogfather ? Well – go and ask him yourself!

Favorite popsicle flavor: You.

Douglas Hackle

Born with one extra finger and two extra toes, Douglas Hackle lives in Northeast Ohio with his wife and son. He attended college at a Jesuit university, abandoned academia after receiving his B.A. in English Literature, accepted a writing-related cubicle job in the business world, and lost his fucking mind somewhere along the way. His first published book, *Clown Tear Junkies*, is a collection of absurdist/bizarro short stories. http://douglashackle.wordpress.com/.

Favorite popsicle flavor: fetal anvil (with clown tears).

Max Booth III

Max Booth III is the editor-in-chief of Perpetual Motion Machine Publishing and the assistant editor of *Dark Moon Digest*. His debut novel, *Toxicity*, will be published in March 2014 by Post Mortem Press. Follow him on Twitter @GiveMeYourTeeth and visit him at http://www.TalesFromTheBooth.com. His favorite popsicle is banana cream. Go ahead, make a joke. Those things are goddamn delicious.

Mercedes M. Yardley

Mercedes M. Yardley is a dark fantasist who wears stilettos and red lipstick. She is the author of the short story collection *Beautiful Sorrows,* the novella *Apocalyptic Montessa and Nuclear Lulu: A Tale of Atomic Love* and her debut novel *Nameless.* Her website is http://www.mercedesyardley.com. Her favorite flavor of popsicle is lime.

James Ward Kirk

James Ward Kirk spends much of his time these days publishing the creative writing of others, and loves doing so. He lives in Indianapolis. James' most recent publication is the anthology *Fresh Fear*, edited by William Cook, and will be releasing *Cellar Door Volume II* in mid-December 2013. His favorite popsicle flavor is orange. Dipped in chocolate. His website is jwkfiction.com.

Sheila Hall

The fingers fly across the keyboard swiftly, focused and full of determination, ideas flowing onto the screen as fast as she can think them. Silhouetted in the dim light she transfers her thoughts into words, creating places and people, ideas and images for the world to see. Her name is Sheila Hall, and she creates stories that make people feel.

A woman of many talents, she stays hidden in the shadows and cloaked in mystery. Yet she's never selfish with her gifts, stepping out into the light to share them with those who need them. Ms. Hall is a riddle that begs to be solved, and the first step to understanding her is reading the tales she tells. Through those you get your first glimpse at the woman behind the words...

Site: http://firesidepress.wordpress.com/
Blog: http://desiresinthedark.wordpress.com/
Twitter: @thedarkerfun
Favorite flavor of popsicle: Banana. No, really.

Rick Austin

Rick Austin, author of *Life Insurance of the Gods* and soon-to-be released *The Naturals,* is a partly-shaven monkey who owns a laptop and insists on using it. He resides both in his own mind and South Africa, but was born in Birmingham, England, where he had a rather good time enjoying the cultural benefits of watching Hong Kong Phooey.

After giving up a wild and unprofitable career serving frozen yoghurt, he embarked upon a life of indulging his favorite hobbies in fashionable nightclubs, where he would gyrate his hips in a way that would make most people blind.

He is currently trying to explain where it all went wrong so that he can do it all over again only with some slight differences. Visit him at http://jn-devsite.com/rickstash/.
Favorite flavor of popsicle: Lemon.

Michael Allen Rose

Michael Allen Rose is a Chicago based writer, musician and performer. He's been published in a variety of strange places including *The Surreal Grotesque*, the *Bizarro Bizarro* anthology and *Fifty Secret Tales of the Whispering Gash: A Queefrotica* as well as having books published by Eraserhead Press and Dynatox Ministries. Flood Damage is the name of his industrial music project. He likes to set things on fire and put on puppet shows when he does readings. He is currently dating a unicorn. He believes that the real conspiracy is born of those who say there is a conspiracy. He likes cats. He likes Indian food. He likes a lot of things, actually. He might even like you. Really. No, not like that. Okay, yeah, like that. Find him at www.michaelallenrose.com and send him presents.

Fave Flavor: Pizza.

Andy de Fonseca

Andy de Fonseca is the author of *The Cheat Code for God Mode* from Eraserhead Press. She is a geek and knows a lot about physics. Her favorite popsicle flavor is wormhole dreamsicle.

Becky Flade

When I was small, I didn't know that not everybody had "stories" in their heads. My parents flipped a coin to decide between anti-psychotics and a typewriter. Luckily for me, the coin landed on typewriter. I've been writing ever since. And while I may not be schizophrenic my favorite popsicle is - the Jolly RancherTM Bomb Pop featuring watermelon, grape, lemon, cherry and green apple stripes. I'd love to have you visit with me on my blog; at any of my online homes; or write to me directly at beckyfladeauthor@gmail.com.

Author Links:
http://beckyfladeauthor.wordpress.com/
https://www.facebook.com/BeckyFlade
https:/witter.com/beckyflade
http://www.goodreads.com/Becky_Flade
http://www.amazon.com/Becky-Flade

Dionne Lister

With two fantasy novels, a collection of suspenseful short stories and a humorous novella that stars a talking vagina called Doris to her writing credits, Dionne loves pushing her writing boundaries. Determined to become a famous author before she is relegated to being a reclusive cat lady, Dionne was super happy to be included in the *Fireside Popsicles* anthology. She is also an editor and copywriter and lives on the eastern seaboard of Down Under, where the poisonous wildlife mean every trip to the garden could be her last. Dionne also finds it weird to write about herself in the third person but does it just to fit in.

Fave Flavor: TimTams.

Gabino Iglesias

Gabino Iglesias is a writer, journalist, and book reviewer living in Austin, TX. He's the author of Gutmouth (Eraserhead Press) and a few other things no one will ever read. His fiction has appeared in Bizarro Central, *Flash Fiction Offensive, Drunken Monkeys, Verbicide*, and a few horror and bizarro anthologies. His nonfiction has appeared in The New York Times, *Verbicide*, The Rumpus,

HTMLGiant, *The Magazine of Bizarro Fiction, Z Magazine, Out of the Gutter, Word Riot*, and a other print and online venues. You can reach him at gabinoiglesias@gmail.com.
Fave Flavor: Mermaid.

Bradley Sands

Bradley Sands wrote the funniest book even in human history known as *TV Snorted my Brain* from LegumeMan Press. Really, you need to read it.
Favorite popsicle flavor: Classified.

Jeremy C. Shipp

Jeremy C. Shipp loves clowns. He loves them so much he wrote a multi-volume omnibus called *Attic Clowns*. He also loves gnomes and bad movies.
Favorite popsicle flavor: Garden Gnome.

Trevor Halliday

Trevor Halliday, born 21st October 1972, in Southend-on-Sea, Essex, England. Creator of the *World of Urutau*, writing has always been a passion. Be it fantasy, horror or poetry. Inspirations include Clive Barker, Michael Moorcock and Tolkien. Favorite flavor of popsicle: Lime!

J.C. Michael

J.C.Michael lives in rural North Yorkshire with his wife, who encourages his writing, and his son, who leaves him little time to get on with it.
His debut novel, *Discoredia*, was released in 2013 by Books of the Dead Press.
As for his favorite Popsicle, or ice lolly if we're going to be English about it, has got to be a strawberry mivvi.

Daniel Vlasaty

Daniel Vlasaty lives in Chicago with his wife and some cats. He works at a methadone clinic. He is the author of the novella *THE CHURCH OF TV AS GOD*, published by Eraserhead Press.
Fave Flavor: Grape.

Troy Blackford

Troy Blackford is a 30-year old writer living in the Twin Cities with his wife, infant son, and two cats. He has eight books available on Amazon and a variety of short stories loose in the wild. He eats more barbecue sauce than you do and he probably reads more than you too, but he doesn't get all stuck up about it. You can find out more about him at http://www.troyblackford.com.

Fave Flavor: BBQ.

Diogenes Ruiz

Diogenes Ruiz was born in the Dominican Republic and grew up in New York City's Washington Heights. A lover of all things sci-fi, he specializes in Christian Fiction. His debut novel, *A Rabbit's Tale: An Easter Story* is followed by *Persistent Evil*, the second installment of a three part saga. "I enjoy writing stories that are unusual and fun to read. I share my faith in Christ through my writing, without being preachy. These stories allow me to ask meaningful questions about beliefs systems, free will, and the classic struggle between good and evil." When not writing, Diogenes is composing music or playing blues guitar at local venues in his hometown of Raleigh, North Carolina.

Fave Flavor: Orange Dreamsicle.

Nikki Guerlain

Nikki Guerlain haunts Portland, Oregon. Her debut novel *Machine Gun Vacation* will be released late 2014 courtesy of Thunderdome Press. Her short stories appear both online and in print. For more information, please go to radwriter.com.

Fave Flavor: Grape.

Baz Nova

If you take a sprinkle of Bukowski, a pinch of Hunter S. Thompson, a smidgen of Dickensian charm and wit, mixed with a healthy dose of varying substances and styles, you will get a much better writer than I.

But as it stands, you get me, Baz NoVa, an unknown nobody from nowheresville. It's cool though, because you can still read my stories and, if it tickles your fancy, follow me on that internet thing we all like so much.

Favourite popsicle flavor: cola (with whiskey, if possible… do they even do them? If not they should).

Jeremy Maddux

Jeremy is the host of the best literary podcast in the world called *Surreal Grotesque*. Anyone who's anyone in the genre of Bizarro fiction can be found right here.

Flavor: Alien (don't judge me).

Pedro Proença

Pedro Proença is a Brazilian public servant, who tries to write sometimes. You can find him at his blog, *The Bizarro World of Pedro* (www.thebizarroworldofpedro.blogspot.com) and on his Facebook page (https://www.facebook.com/punksterbass). He lives in Rio de Janeiro with his family (wife, parents and grandparents).

Pedro's favorite popsicle flavor is Brazilian passion fruit.

M.C. O'Neill

M.C. is arguably sane, but the State has never put him where he belongs - an asylum.

Alternating between touching YA tales of solipsistic fantasy and Bizarro-fueled filth, O'Neill has little instinct for business. This is not a problem.

It's quite possible that his cheese is sliding off his cracker, but he cares for this not.

As the co-editor for Fireside Press, M.C. works like a chimp to provide fine anthologies which delve into the odd and absurd for other writers who don't have a home.

He claims his heroes are James Gunn, Ernest Borgnine and Soupy Sails.

His favorite flavor of popsicle is chicken.

Emily Stern

Emily Stern is a MYLF, a writer, and a teacher, originally from the Southside of Chicago and currently residing in Santa Fe, NM. *Mellow Yellow*, is a piece of nonfiction that she hopes is even better than the 1984-not-at-all-a-hit-movie *Angel*, which, had she seen it prior to this story's situation, she would have charged so much more. Emily's book, *Wild, Wild Horses—A Memoir*, about her childhood and her mother's death from AIDS 1993, is currently being shopped.

She has been writing, performing, and teaching for over twenty years- credits include: The Sex Worker's Art Show National Tour, The Transfused, Ladyfest Olympia and Los Angeles, *The Portland Review*, *Make/Shift Magazine*, The Femmolition Derby, Wise Fool New Mexico, Santa Fe Art Institute, and The Rock and Roll Camp for Girls. She has an MFA from Goddard College in Creative Nonfiction with a critical emphasis on women and AIDS in literature. She teaches at Santa Fe Community College, Santa Fe University of Art and Design, and the Institute of American Indian Arts.

Since she resides in New Mexico, it can only be assumed her favorite popsicle flavor is Green Chile.

M.J. Sydney

M.J. is an author of fine horror and suspense fiction. We at Fireside Press know what the initials stand for, and it isn't Mary Jane, in case you were wondering.

Her favorite popsicle flavor is blood.

Thank you for enjoying FIRESIDE POPSICLES. We at Fireside Press will deliver more literary goodness in the future, so be on the lookout.

And remember: Friends don't let friends use their asses for a flamethrower.

www.ingramcontent.com/pod-product-compliance
Lightning Source LLC
Chambersburg PA
CBHW080902120626
46555CB00008B/2916